MARVEL

MARVEL ACTION SPIDER-MAN

A NEW BEGINNING

Marvel Publishing:

Jeff Youngquist: VP Production & Special Projects
Caitlin O'Connell: Assistant Editor, Special Projects
Sven Larsen: Director, Licensed Publishing
David Gabriel: SVP Print, Sales & Marketing
C.B. Cebulski: Editor In Chief
Joe Quesada: Chief Creative Officer
Dan Buckley: President, Marvel Entertainment
Alan Fine: Executive Producer

IDW Publishing:

IDW

Collection Edits
JUSTIN EISINGER
and **ALONZO SIMON**

Production Assistance
SHAWN LEE

Cover Art by
GABRIEL RODRIGUEZ

Cover Colors by
NELSON DANIEL

Chris Ryall, President and Publisher/CCO
Cara Morrison, Chief Financial Officer
Matt Ruzicka, Chief Accounting Officer
David Hedgecock, Associate Publisher
John Barber, Editor-In-Chief
Justin Eisinger, Editorial Director, Graphic Novels & Collections
Jerry Bennington, VP of New Product Development
Lorelei Bunjes, VP of Technology & Information Services
Jud Meyers, Sales Director
Anna Morrow, Marketing Director
Tara McCrillis, Director of Design & Production
Mike Ford, Director of Operations
Rebekah Cahalin, General Manager

Ted Adams and Robbie Robbins, IDW Founders

ISBN: 978-1-68405-514-2   22 21 20 19   3 4 5 6

Special thanks: **Tom Brevoort**, **Nick Lowe**, and **Sana Amanat**

Originally published as MARVEL ACTION: SPIDER-MAN issues #1–3.

For international rights, contact licensing@idwpublishing.com

MARVEL

MARVEL ACTION SPIDER-MAN

A NEW BEGINNING

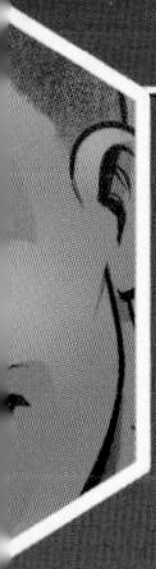

WRITTEN BY DELILAH S. DAWSON

ART BY FICO OSSIO

COLORS BY RONDA PATTISON

LETTERS BY SHAWN LEE

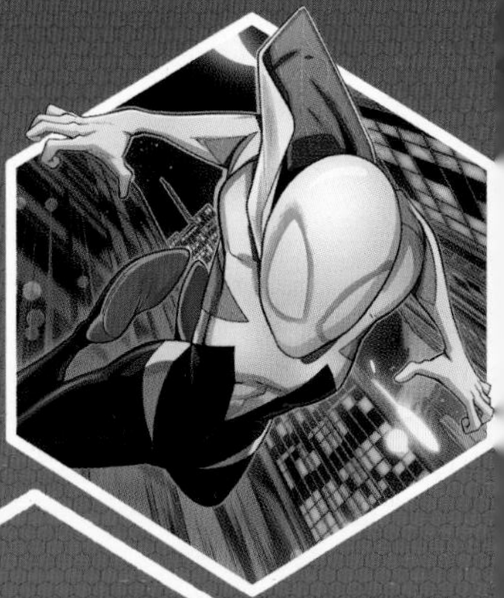

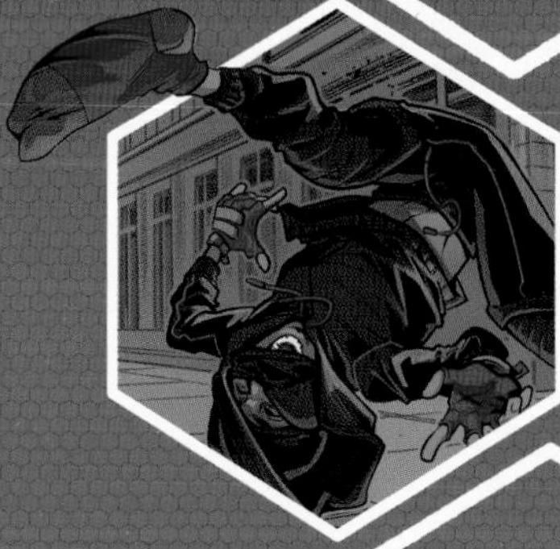

ASSISTANT EDITORS ANNI PERHEENTUPA & ELIZABETH BREI

ASSOCIATE EDITOR CHASE MAROTZ

EDITOR DENTON J. TIPTON

EDITOR IN CHIEF JOHN BARBER

SPIDER-MAN CREATED BY STAN LEE & STEVE DITKO

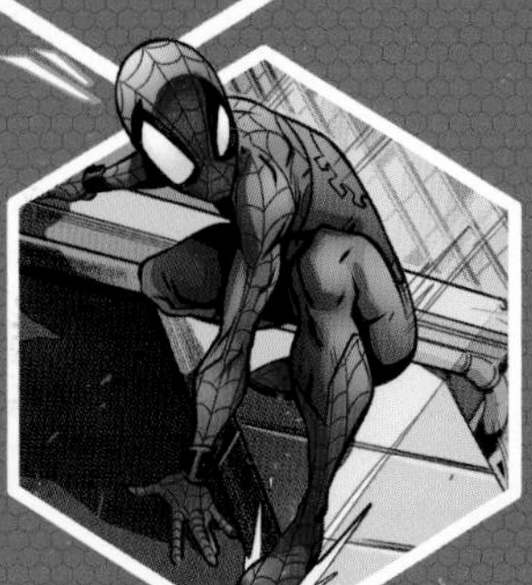

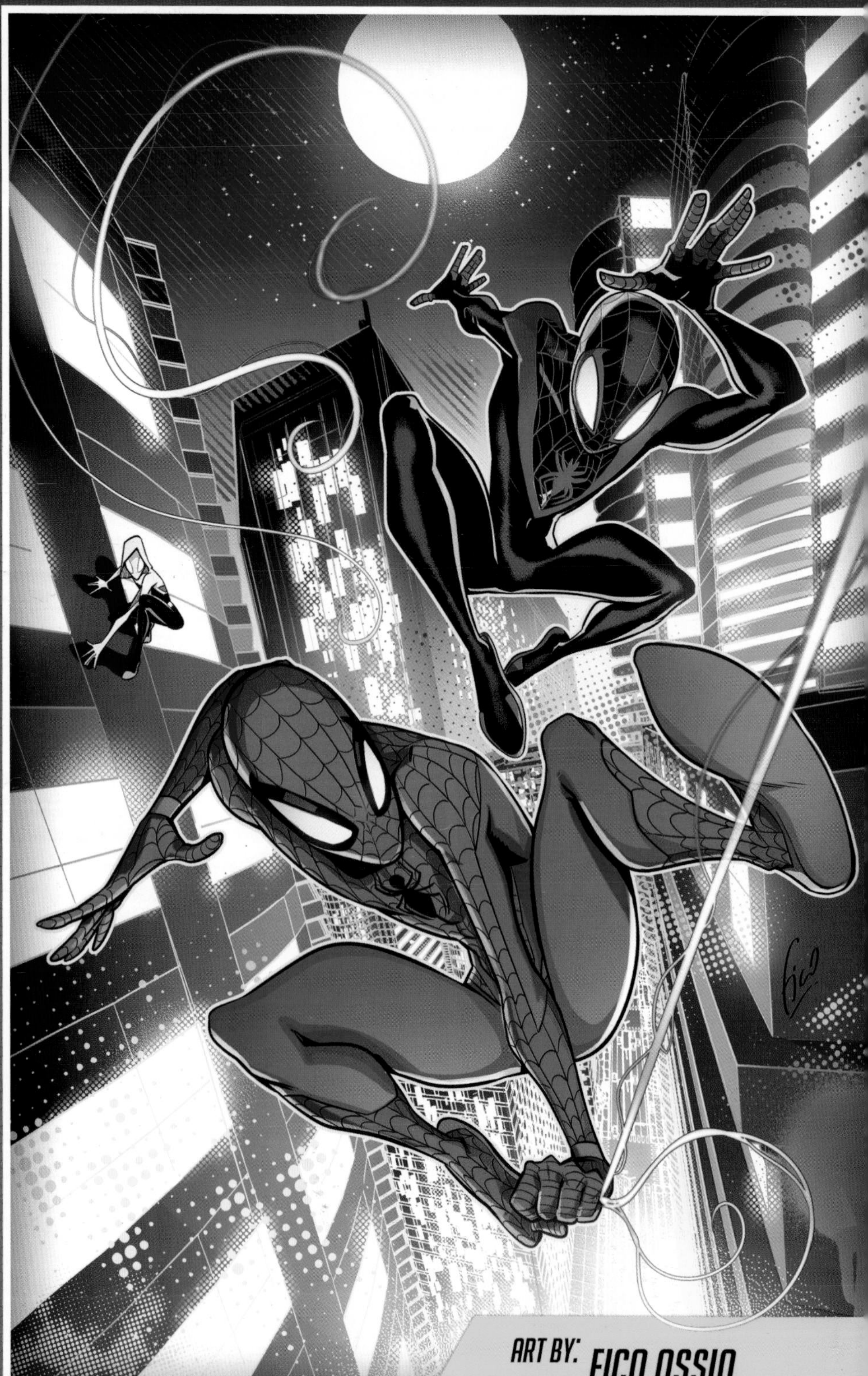

ART BY: FICO OSSIO

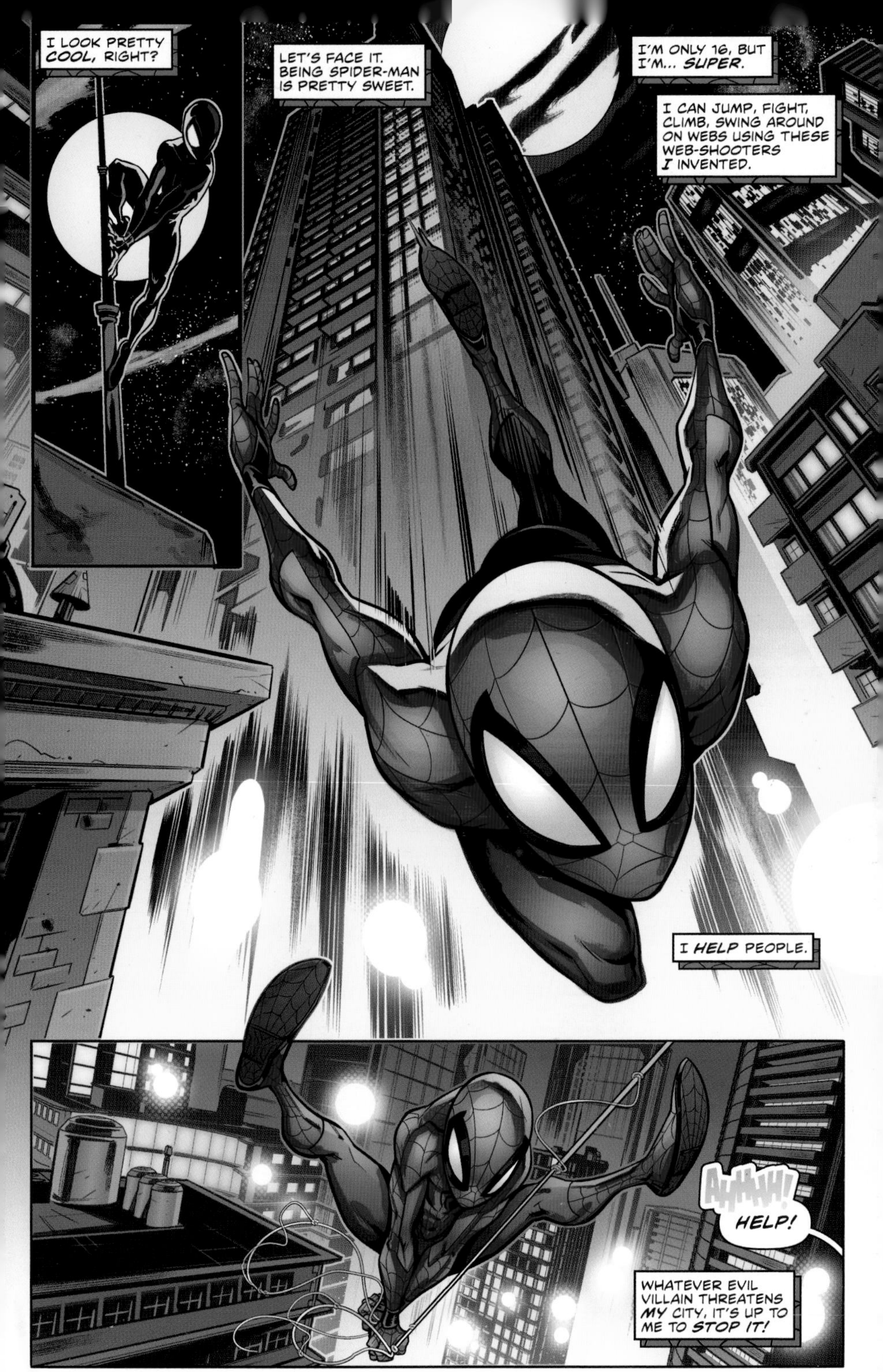
I LOOK PRETTY COOL, RIGHT?
LET'S FACE IT. BEING SPIDER-MAN IS PRETTY SWEET.
I'M ONLY 16, BUT I'M... SUPER.
I CAN JUMP, FIGHT, CLIMB, SWING AROUND ON WEBS USING THESE WEB-SHOOTERS I INVENTED.
I HELP PEOPLE.
AHHHH! HELP!
WHATEVER EVIL VILLAIN THREATENS MY CITY, IT'S UP TO ME TO STOP IT!

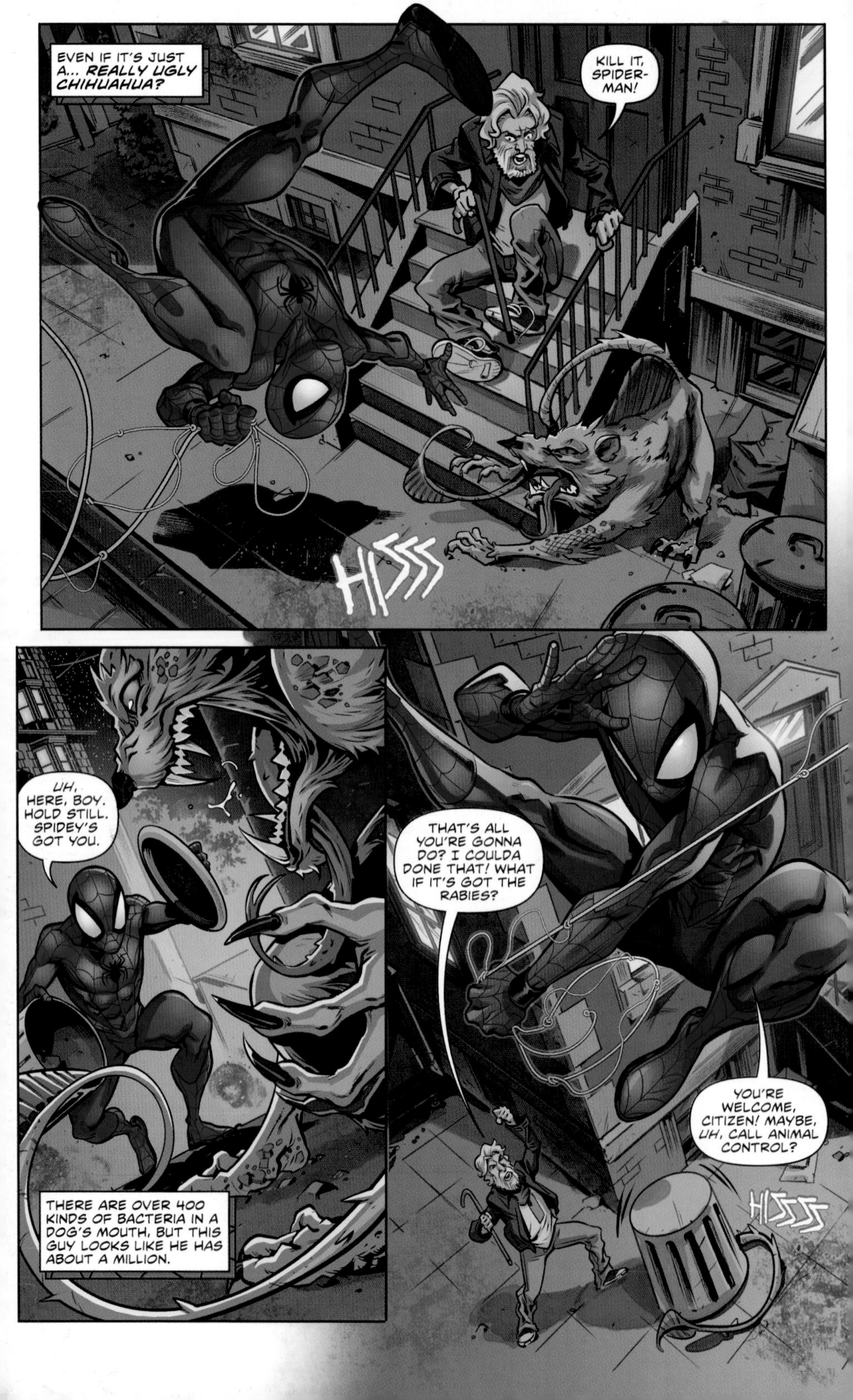
EVEN IF IT'S JUST A... REALLY UGLY CHIHUAHUA?
KILL IT, SPIDER-MAN!
HISSS
UH, HERE, BOY. HOLD STILL. SPIDEY'S GOT YOU.
THERE ARE OVER 400 KINDS OF BACTERIA IN A DOG'S MOUTH, BUT THIS GUY LOOKS LIKE HE HAS ABOUT A MILLION.
THAT'S ALL YOU'RE GONNA DO? I COULDA DONE THAT! WHAT IF IT'S GOT THE RABIES?
YOU'RE WELCOME, CITIZEN! MAYBE, UH, CALL ANIMAL CONTROL?
HISSS

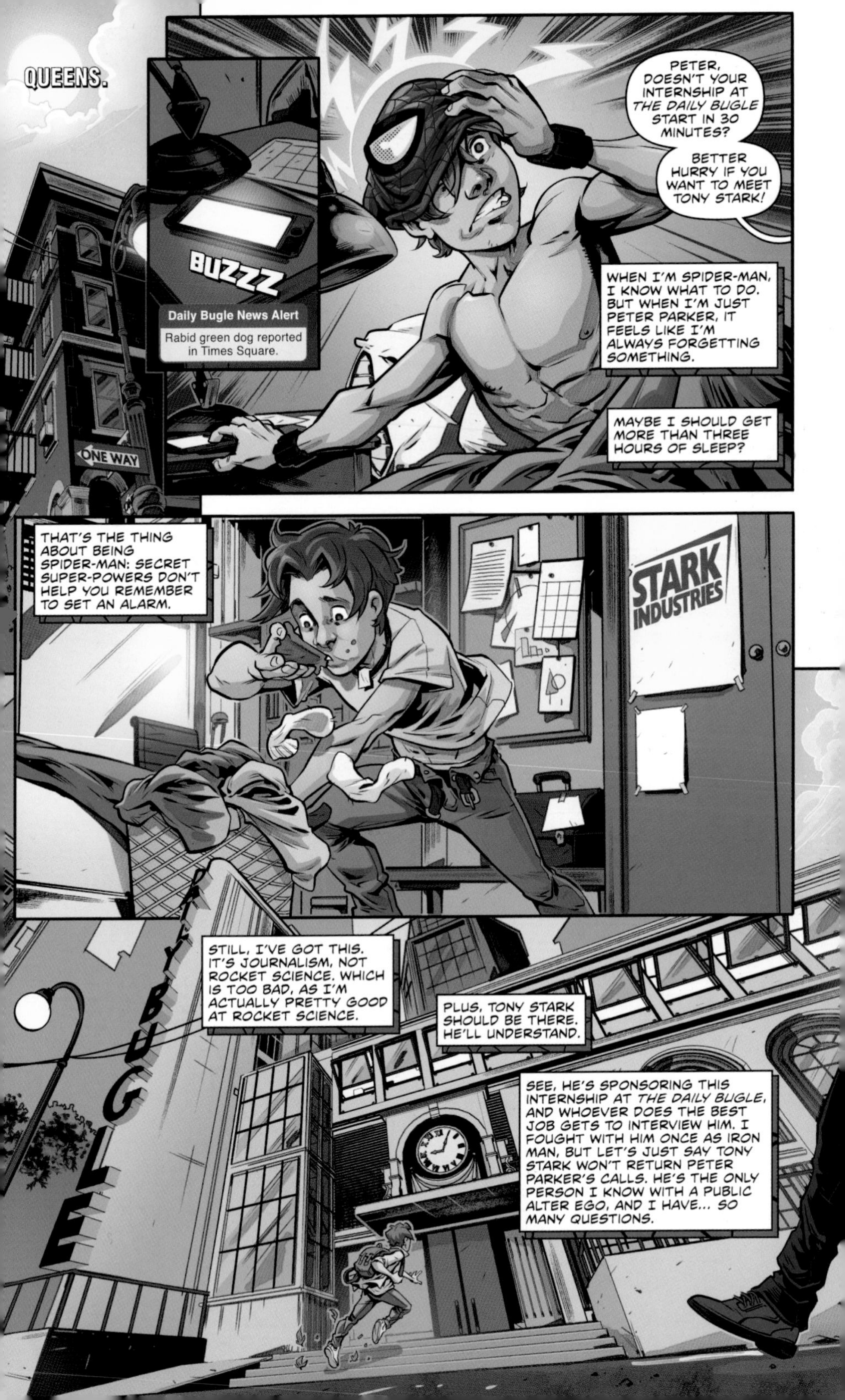
QUEENS.
BUZZZ
Daily Bugle News Alert
Rabid green dog reported in Times Square.
PETER, DOESN'T YOUR INTERNSHIP AT THE DAILY BUGLE START IN 30 MINUTES?
BETTER HURRY IF YOU WANT TO MEET TONY STARK!
WHEN I'M SPIDER-MAN, I KNOW WHAT TO DO. BUT WHEN I'M JUST PETER PARKER, IT FEELS LIKE I'M ALWAYS FORGETTING SOMETHING.
MAYBE I SHOULD GET MORE THAN THREE HOURS OF SLEEP?
ONE WAY
THAT'S THE THING ABOUT BEING SPIDER-MAN: SECRET SUPER-POWERS DON'T HELP YOU REMEMBER TO SET AN ALARM.
STARK INDUSTRIES
STILL, I'VE GOT THIS. IT'S JOURNALISM, NOT ROCKET SCIENCE. WHICH IS TOO BAD, AS I'M ACTUALLY PRETTY GOOD AT ROCKET SCIENCE.
PLUS, TONY STARK SHOULD BE THERE. HE'LL UNDERSTAND.
SEE, HE'S SPONSORING THIS INTERNSHIP AT THE DAILY BUGLE, AND WHOEVER DOES THE BEST JOB GETS TO INTERVIEW HIM. I FOUGHT WITH HIM ONCE AS IRON MAN, BUT LET'S JUST SAY TONY STARK WON'T RETURN PETER PARKER'S CALLS. HE'S THE ONLY PERSON I KNOW WITH A PUBLIC ALTER EGO, AND I HAVE... SO MANY QUESTIONS.

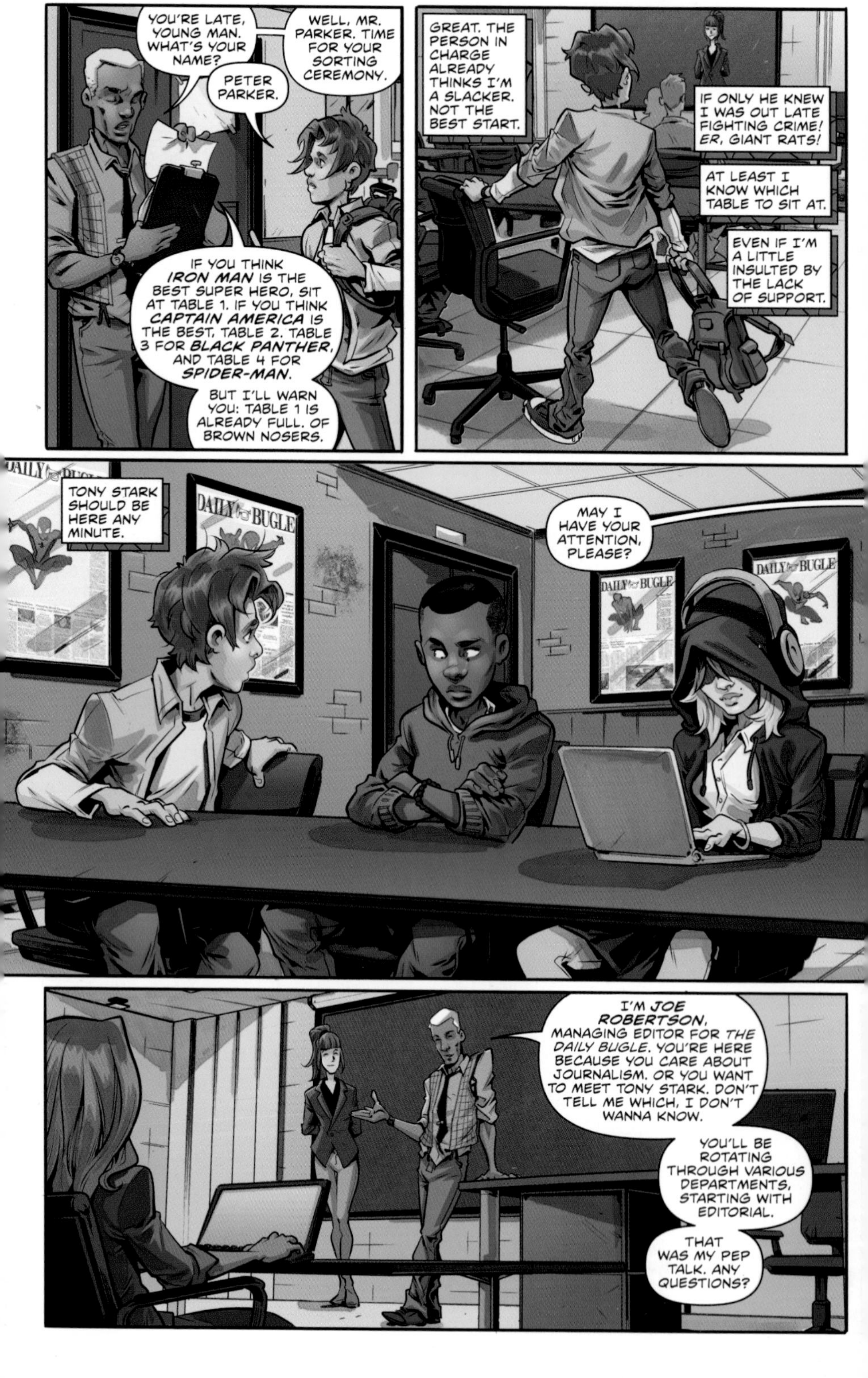
YOU'RE LATE, YOUNG MAN. WHAT'S YOUR NAME?
PETER PARKER.
WELL, MR. PARKER. TIME FOR YOUR SORTING CEREMONY.
IF YOU THINK *IRON MAN* IS THE BEST SUPER HERO, SIT AT TABLE 1. IF YOU THINK *CAPTAIN AMERICA* IS THE BEST, TABLE 2. TABLE 3 FOR *BLACK PANTHER*, AND TABLE 4 FOR *SPIDER-MAN*.
BUT I'LL WARN YOU: TABLE 1 IS ALREADY FULL. OF BROWN NOSERS.
GREAT. THE PERSON IN CHARGE ALREADY THINKS I'M A SLACKER. NOT THE BEST START.
IF ONLY HE KNEW I WAS OUT LATE FIGHTING CRIME! ER, GIANT RATS!
AT LEAST I KNOW WHICH TABLE TO SIT AT.
EVEN IF I'M A LITTLE INSULTED BY THE LACK OF SUPPORT.
TONY STARK SHOULD BE HERE ANY MINUTE.
MAY I HAVE YOUR ATTENTION, PLEASE?
DAILY BUGLE
I'M *JOE ROBERTSON*, MANAGING EDITOR FOR *THE DAILY BUGLE*. YOU'RE HERE BECAUSE YOU CARE ABOUT JOURNALISM. OR YOU WANT TO MEET TONY STARK. DON'T TELL ME WHICH, I DON'T WANNA KNOW.
YOU'LL BE ROTATING THROUGH VARIOUS DEPARTMENTS, STARTING WITH EDITORIAL.
THAT WAS MY PEP TALK. ANY QUESTIONS?

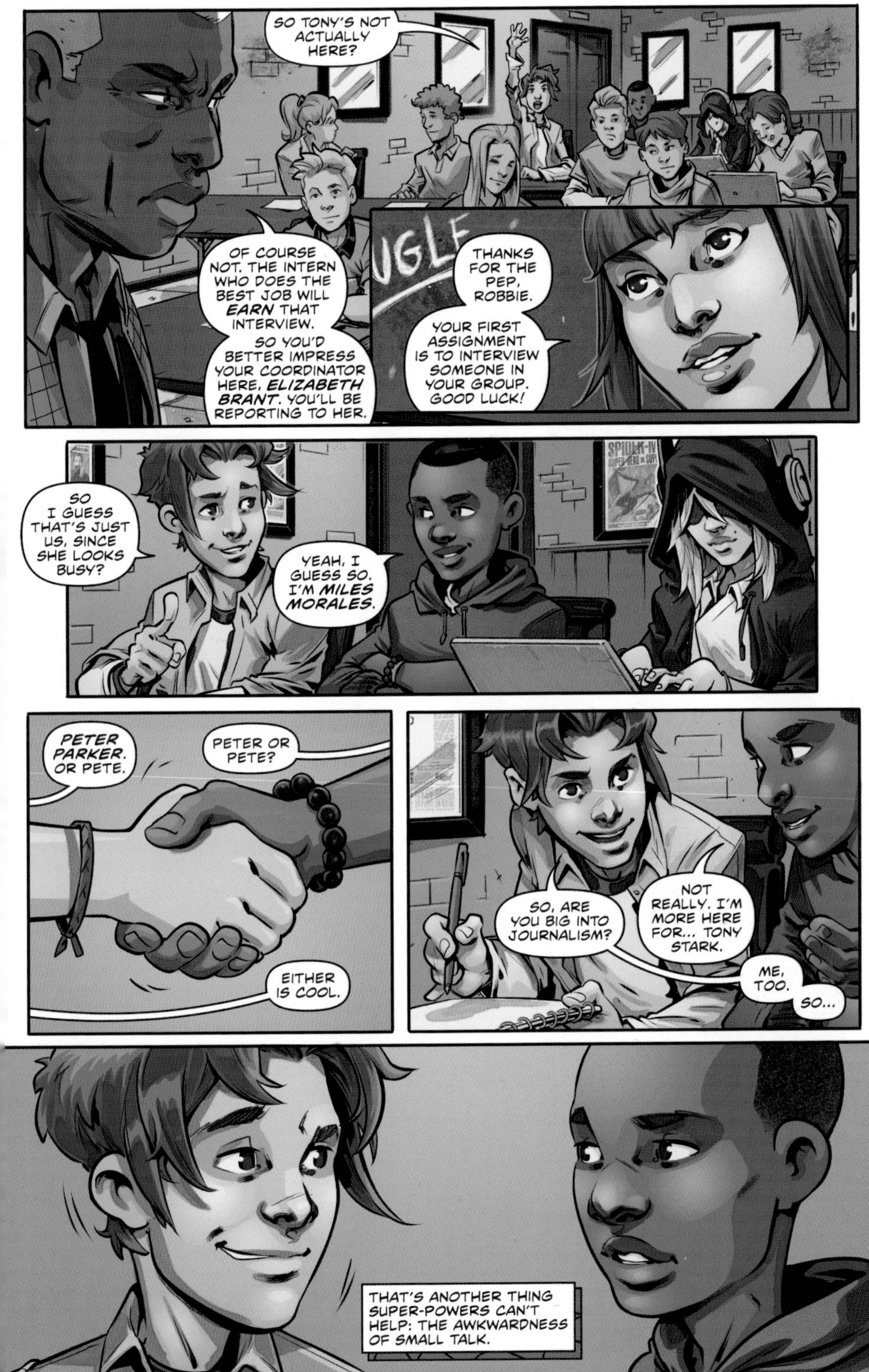
SO TONY'S NOT ACTUALLY HERE?
OF COURSE NOT. THE INTERN WHO DOES THE BEST JOB WILL EARN THAT INTERVIEW.
SO YOU'D BETTER IMPRESS YOUR COORDINATOR HERE, ELIZABETH BRANT. YOU'LL BE REPORTING TO HER.
UGLE
THANKS FOR THE PEP, ROBBIE.
YOUR FIRST ASSIGNMENT IS TO INTERVIEW SOMEONE IN YOUR GROUP. GOOD LUCK!
SO I GUESS THAT'S JUST US, SINCE SHE LOOKS BUSY?
YEAH, I GUESS SO. I'M MILES MORALES.
PETER PARKER. OR PETE.
PETER OR PETE?
EITHER IS COOL.
SO, ARE YOU BIG INTO JOURNALISM?
NOT REALLY. I'M MORE HERE FOR... TONY STARK.
ME, TOO.
SO...
THAT'S ANOTHER THING SUPER-POWERS CAN'T HELP: THE AWKWARDNESS OF SMALL TALK.

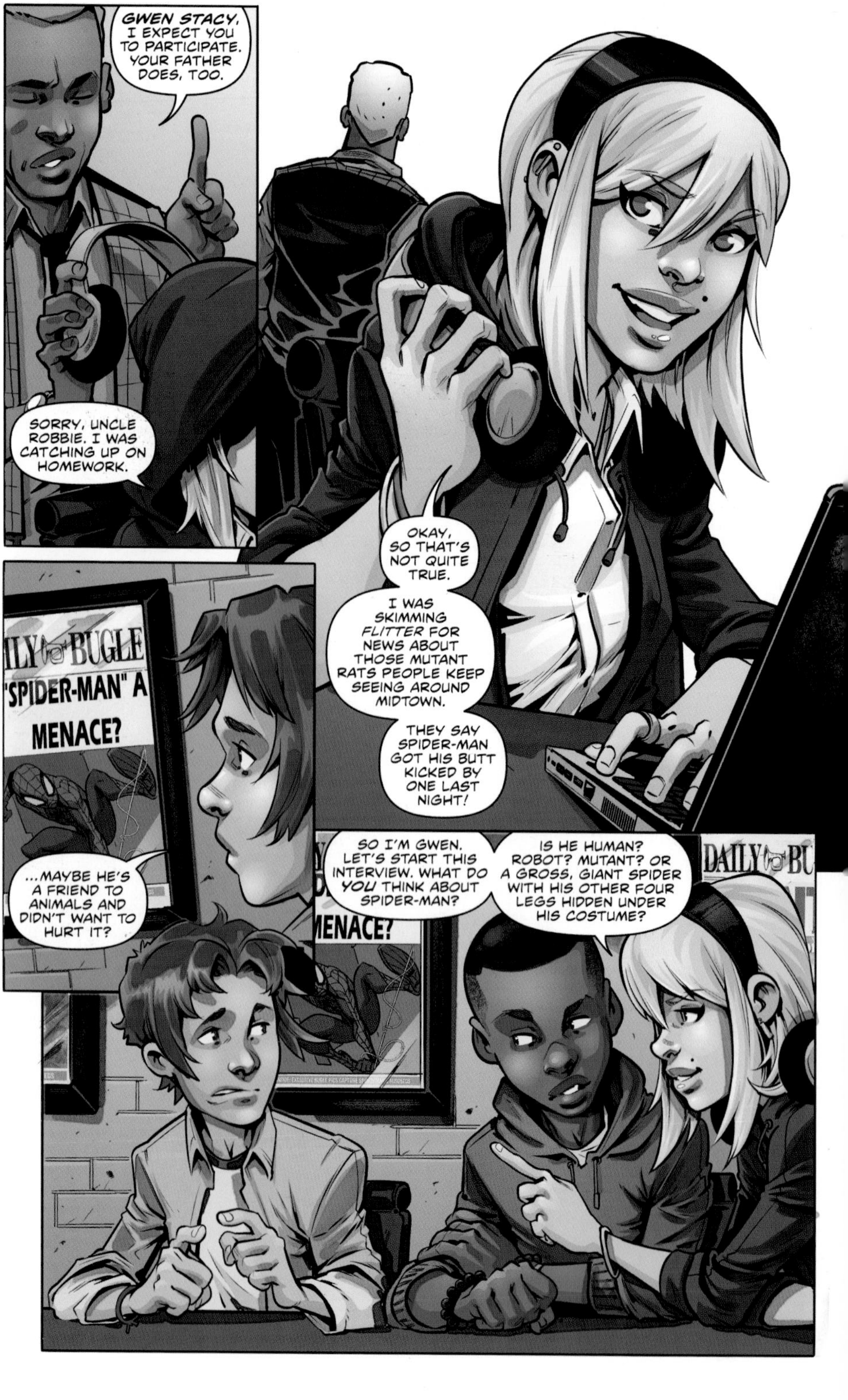
GWEN STACY, I EXPECT YOU TO PARTICIPATE. YOUR FATHER DOES, TOO.
SORRY, UNCLE ROBBIE. I WAS CATCHING UP ON HOMEWORK.
OKAY, SO THAT'S NOT QUITE TRUE.
I WAS SKIMMING *FLITTER* FOR NEWS ABOUT THOSE MUTANT RATS PEOPLE KEEP SEEING AROUND MIDTOWN.
THEY SAY SPIDER-MAN GOT HIS BUTT KICKED BY ONE LAST NIGHT!
...MAYBE HE'S A FRIEND TO ANIMALS AND DIDN'T WANT TO HURT IT?
SO I'M GWEN. LET'S START THIS INTERVIEW. WHAT DO *YOU* THINK ABOUT SPIDER-MAN?
IS HE HUMAN? ROBOT? MUTANT? OR A GROSS, GIANT SPIDER WITH HIS OTHER FOUR LEGS HIDDEN UNDER HIS COSTUME?

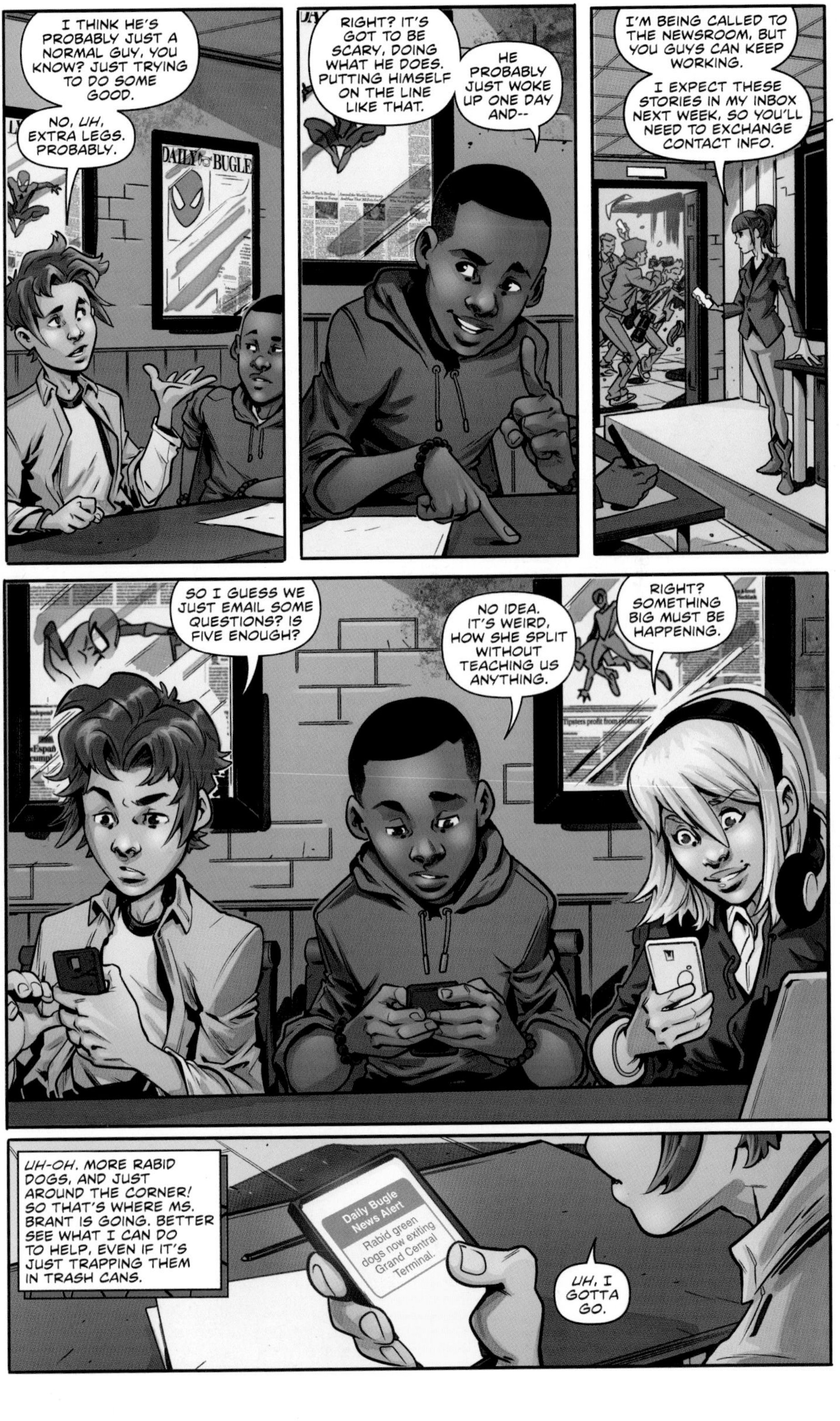
I THINK HE'S PROBABLY JUST A NORMAL GUY, YOU KNOW? JUST TRYING TO DO SOME GOOD.
NO, *UH*, EXTRA LEGS. PROBABLY.
DAILY BUGLE
RIGHT? IT'S GOT TO BE SCARY, DOING WHAT HE DOES. PUTTING HIMSELF ON THE LINE LIKE THAT.
HE PROBABLY JUST WOKE UP ONE DAY AND--
I'M BEING CALLED TO THE NEWSROOM, BUT YOU GUYS CAN KEEP WORKING.
I EXPECT THESE STORIES IN MY INBOX NEXT WEEK, SO YOU'LL NEED TO EXCHANGE CONTACT INFO.
SO I GUESS WE JUST EMAIL SOME QUESTIONS? IS FIVE ENOUGH?
NO IDEA. IT'S WEIRD, HOW SHE SPLIT WITHOUT TEACHING US ANYTHING.
RIGHT? SOMETHING BIG MUST BE HAPPENING.
UH-OH. MORE RABID DOGS, AND JUST AROUND THE CORNER! SO THAT'S WHERE MS. BRANT IS GOING. BETTER SEE WHAT I CAN DO TO HELP, EVEN IF IT'S JUST TRAPPING THEM IN TRASH CANS.
Daily Bugle News Alert
Rabid green dogs now exiting Grand Central Terminal.
UH, I GOTTA GO.

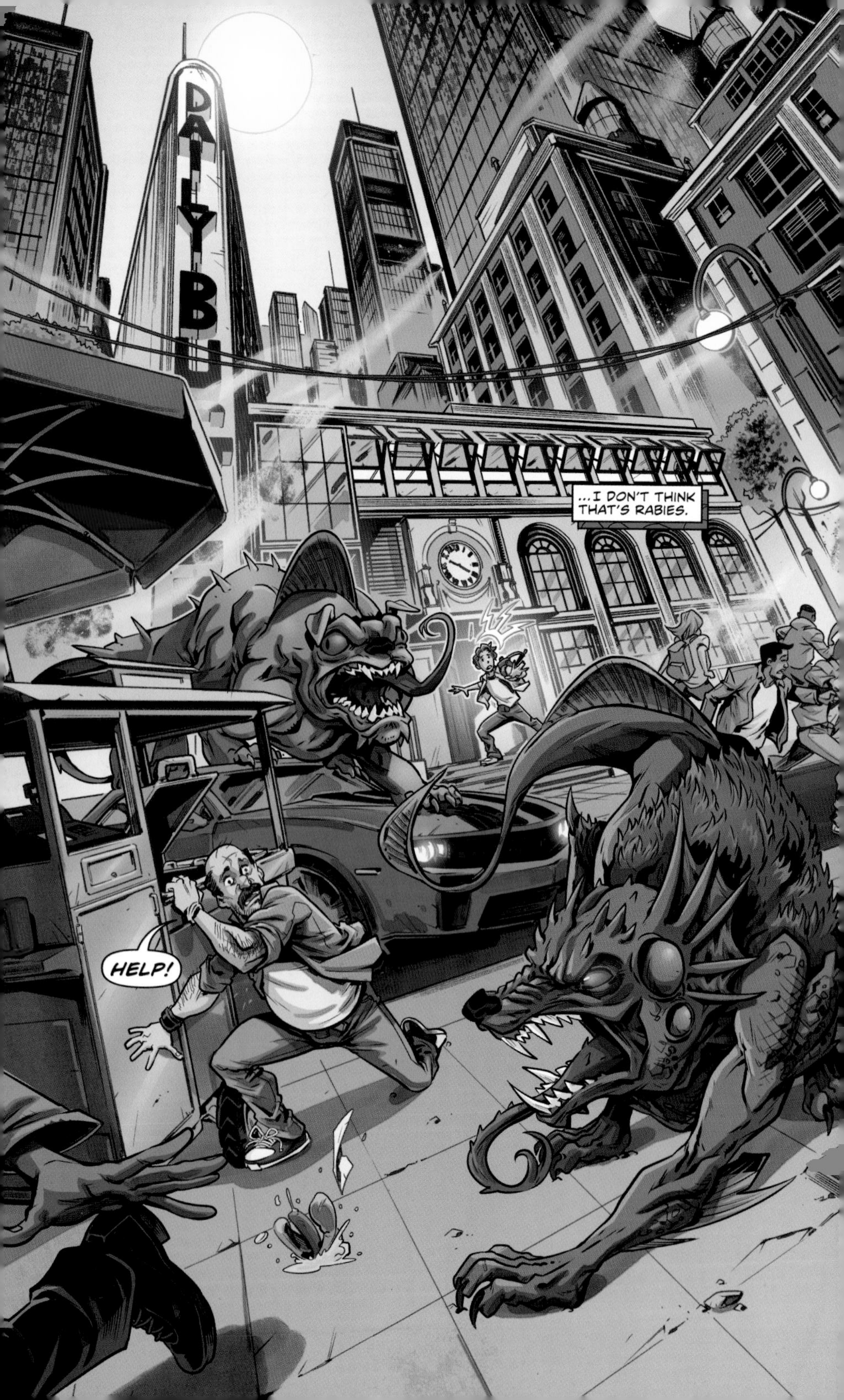
DAILY BU
...I DON'T THINK THAT'S RABIES.
HELP!

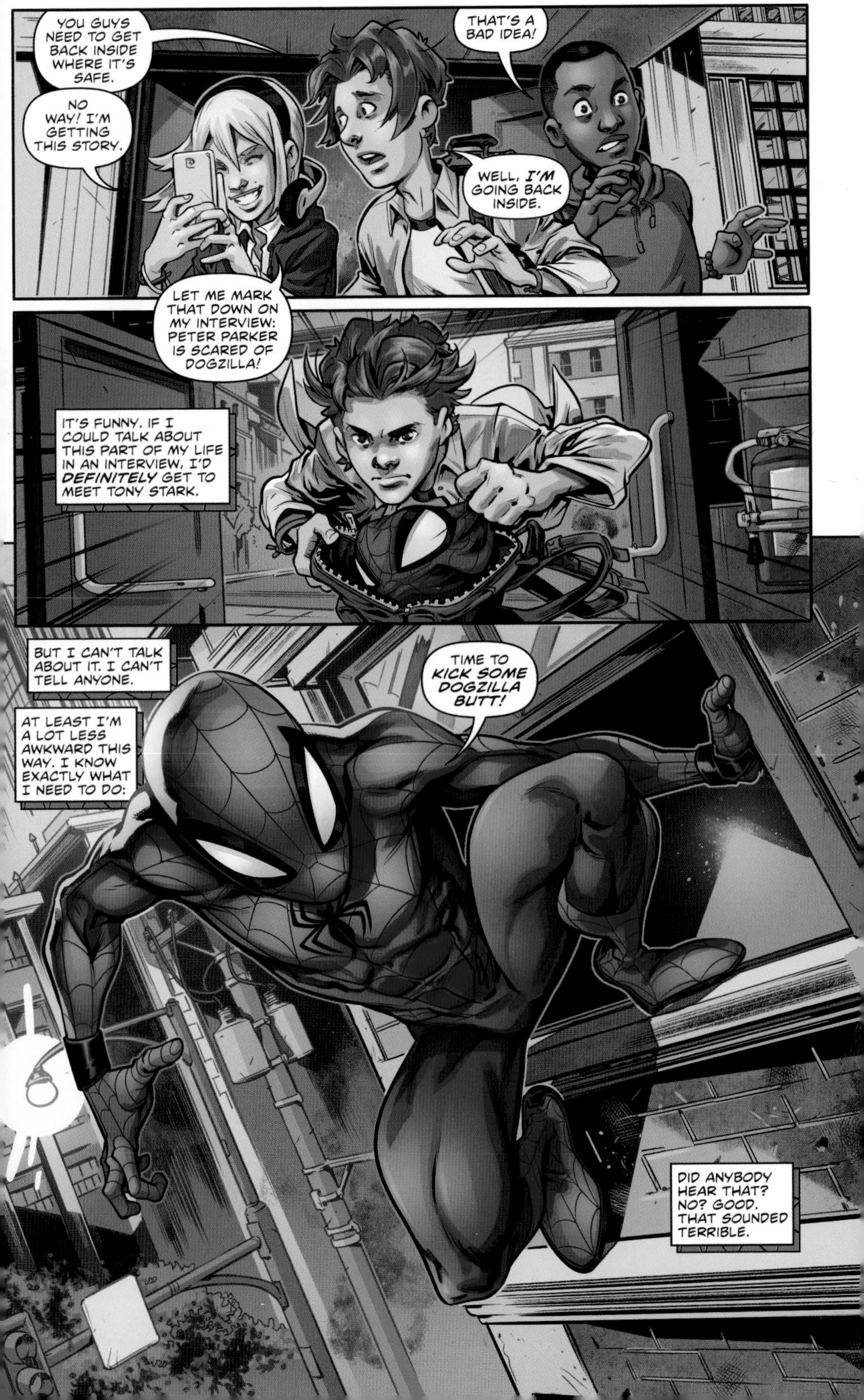
YOU GUYS NEED TO GET BACK INSIDE WHERE IT'S SAFE.
NO WAY! I'M GETTING THIS STORY.
THAT'S A BAD IDEA!
WELL, I'M GOING BACK INSIDE.
LET ME MARK THAT DOWN ON MY INTERVIEW: PETER PARKER IS SCARED OF DOGZILLA!
IT'S FUNNY. IF I COULD TALK ABOUT THIS PART OF MY LIFE IN AN INTERVIEW, I'D DEFINITELY GET TO MEET TONY STARK.
BUT I CAN'T TALK ABOUT IT. I CAN'T TELL ANYONE.
AT LEAST I'M A LOT LESS AWKWARD THIS WAY. I KNOW EXACTLY WHAT I NEED TO DO:
TIME TO KICK SOME DOGZILLA BUTT!
DID ANYBODY HEAR THAT? NO? GOOD. THAT SOUNDED TERRIBLE.

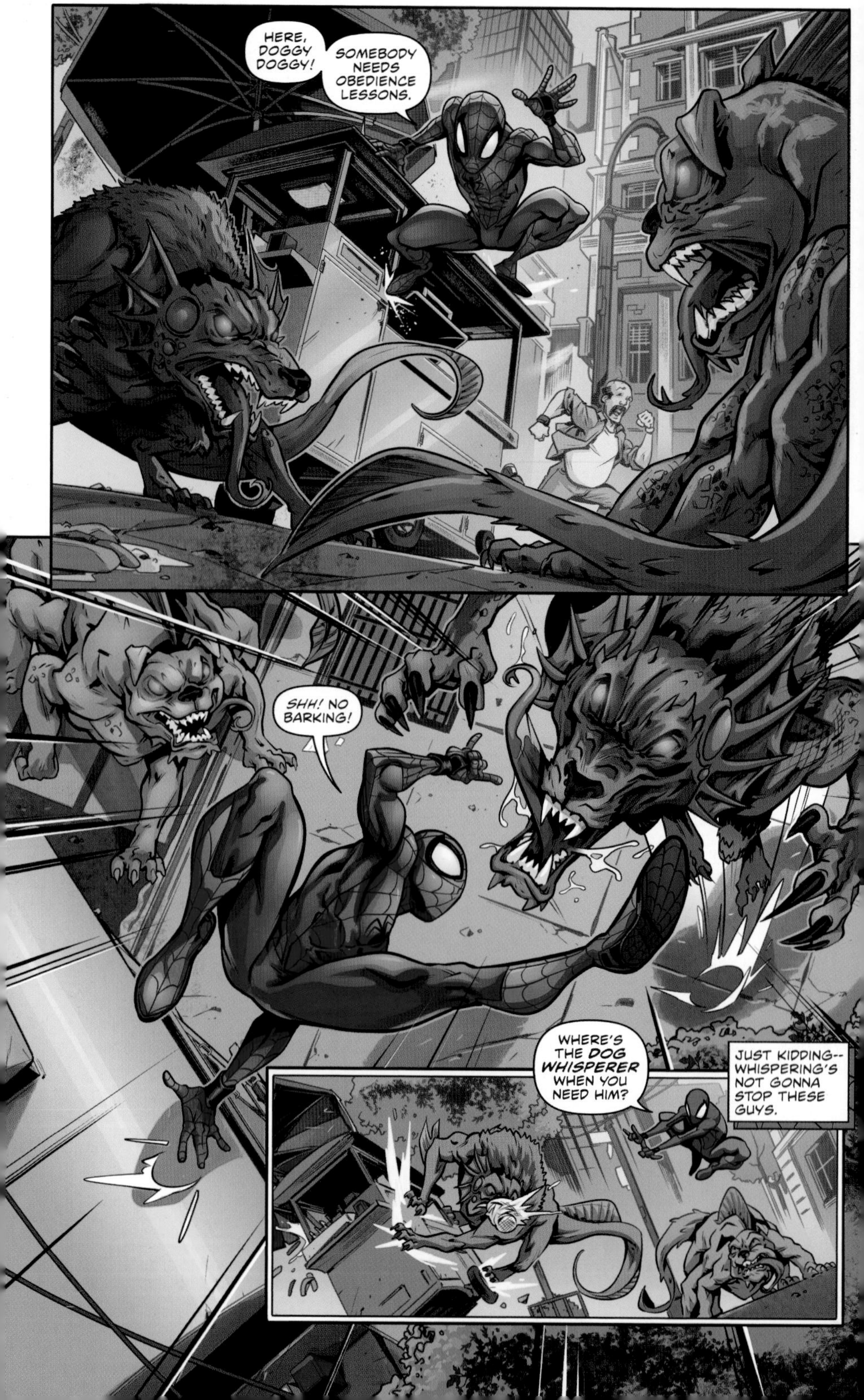

HERE, DOGGY DOGGY!
SOMEBODY NEEDS OBEDIENCE LESSONS.
SHH! NO BARKING!
WHERE'S THE DOG WHISPERER WHEN YOU NEED HIM?
JUST KIDDING-- WHISPERING'S NOT GONNA STOP THESE GUYS.

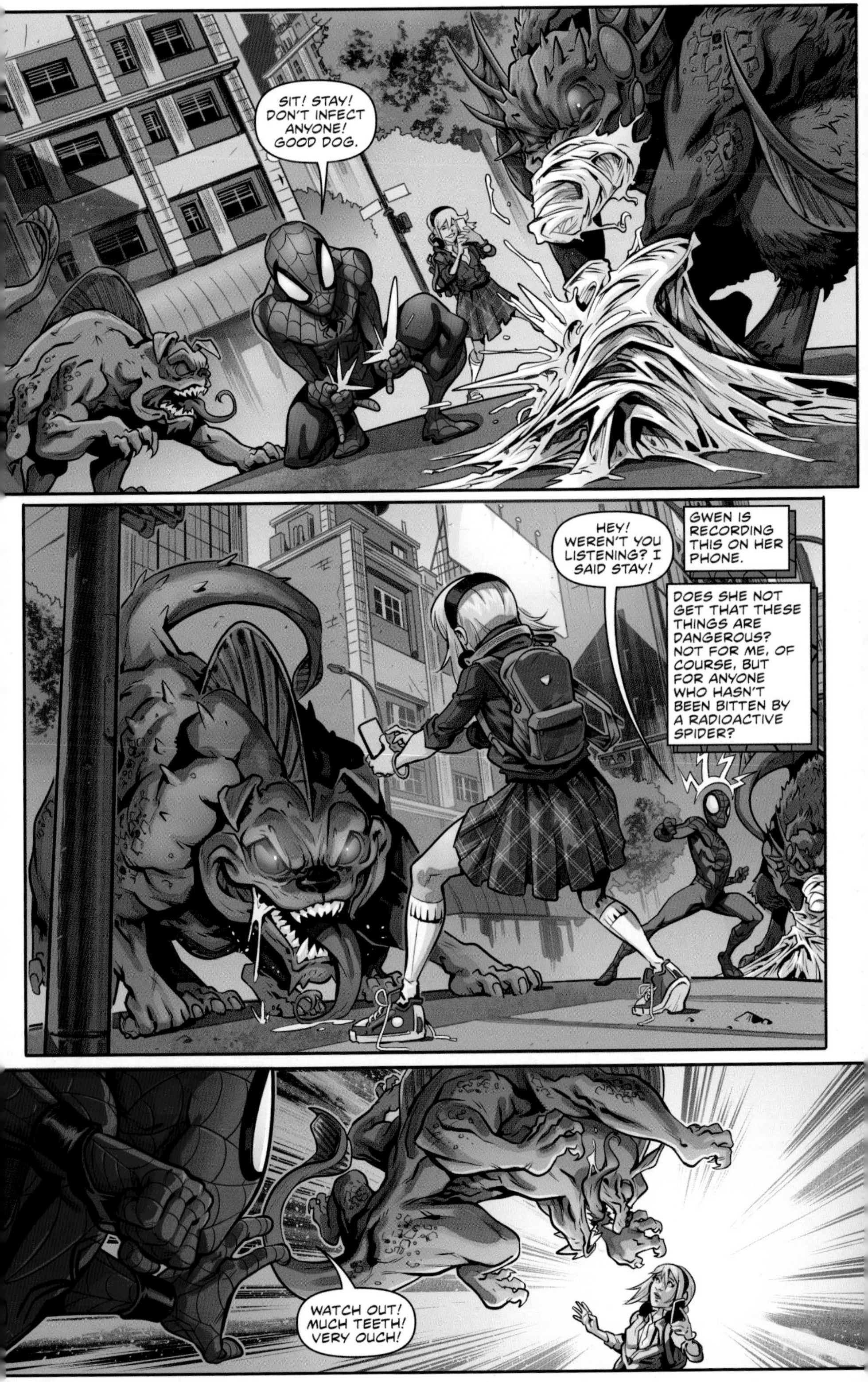
SIT! STAY! DON'T INFECT ANYONE! GOOD DOG.
HEY! WEREN'T YOU LISTENING? I SAID STAY!
GWEN IS RECORDING THIS ON HER PHONE.
DOES SHE NOT GET THAT THESE THINGS ARE DANGEROUS? NOT FOR ME, OF COURSE, BUT FOR ANYONE WHO HASN'T BEEN BITTEN BY A RADIOACTIVE SPIDER?
WATCH OUT! MUCH TEETH! VERY OUCH!

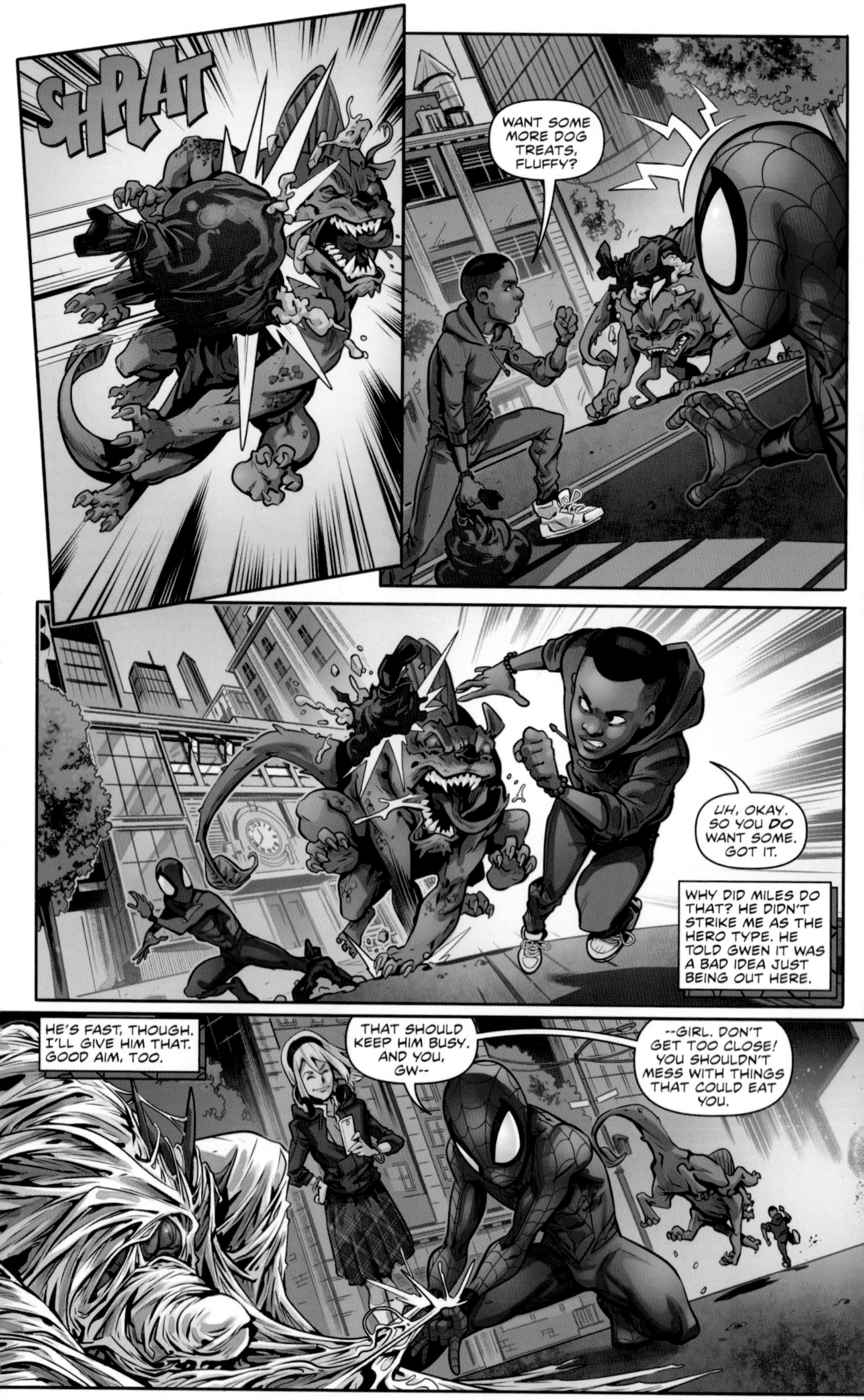

SHRAT
WANT SOME MORE DOG TREATS, FLUFFY?
UH, OKAY. SO YOU DO WANT SOME. GOT IT.
WHY DID MILES DO THAT? HE DIDN'T STRIKE ME AS THE HERO TYPE. HE TOLD GWEN IT WAS A BAD IDEA JUST BEING OUT HERE.
HE'S FAST, THOUGH. I'LL GIVE HIM THAT. GOOD AIM, TOO.
THAT SHOULD KEEP HIM BUSY. AND YOU, GW--
--GIRL. DON'T GET TOO CLOSE! YOU SHOULDN'T MESS WITH THINGS THAT COULD EAT YOU.

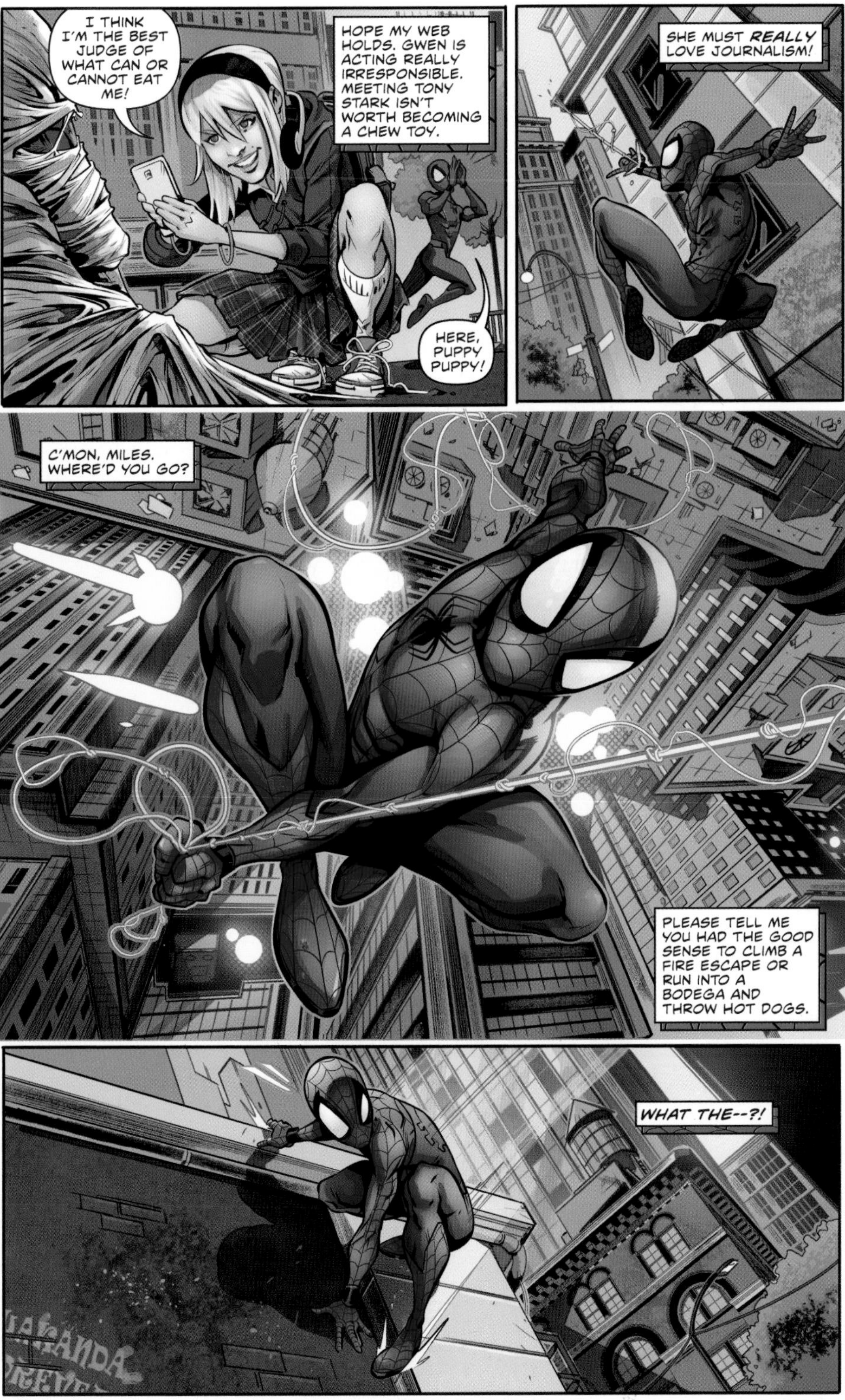

I THINK I'M THE BEST JUDGE OF WHAT CAN OR CANNOT EAT ME!
HOPE MY WEB HOLDS. GWEN IS ACTING REALLY IRRESPONSIBLE. MEETING TONY STARK ISN'T WORTH BECOMING A CHEW TOY.
HERE, PUPPY PUPPY!
SHE MUST REALLY LOVE JOURNALISM!
C'MON, MILES. WHERE'D YOU GO?
PLEASE TELL ME YOU HAD THE GOOD SENSE TO CLIMB A FIRE ESCAPE OR RUN INTO A BODEGA AND THROW HOT DOGS.
WHAT THE--?!

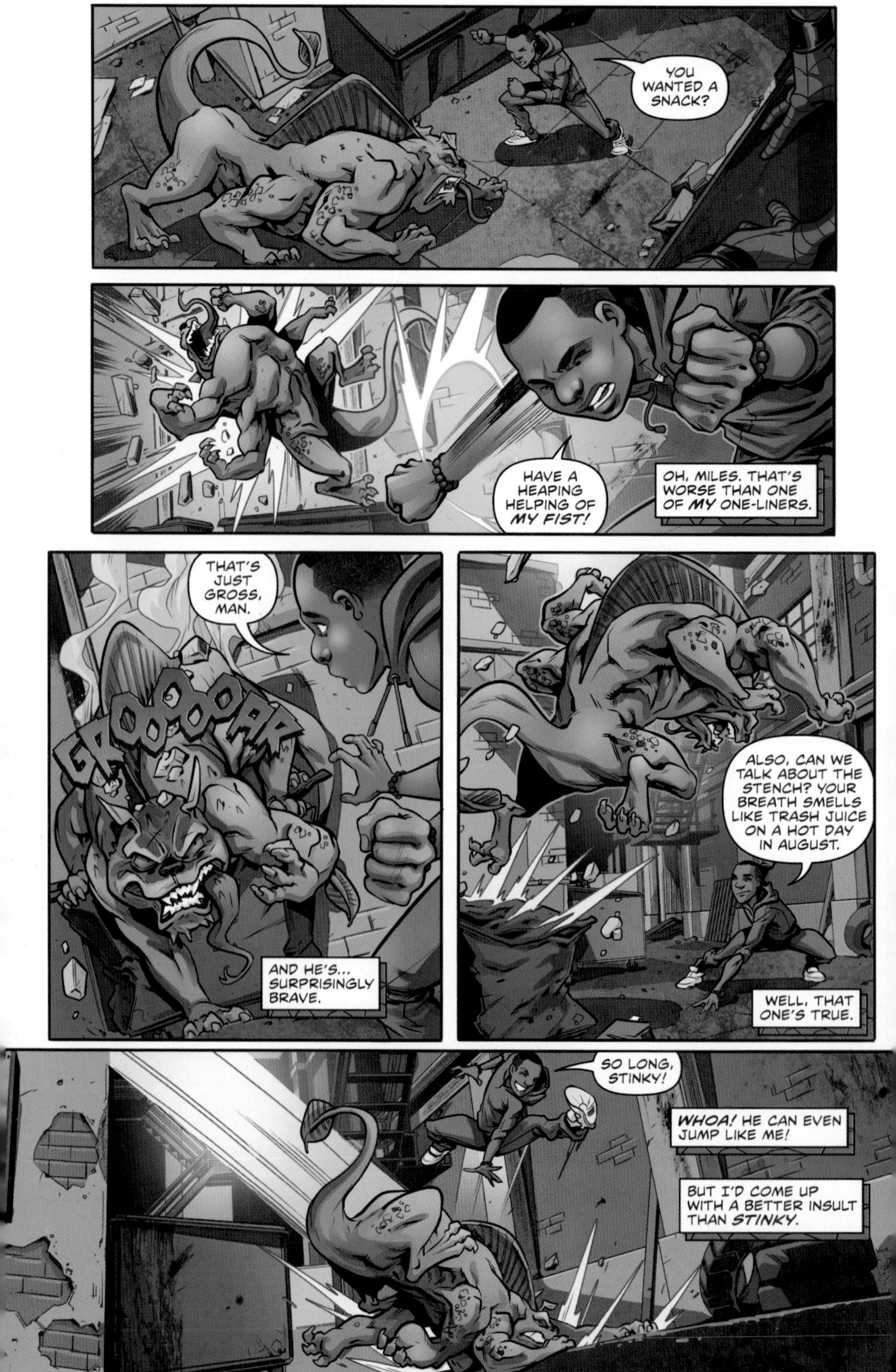
YOU WANTED A SNACK?
HAVE A HEAPING HELPING OF *MY FIST!*
OH, MILES. THAT'S WORSE THAN ONE OF *MY* ONE-LINERS.
THAT'S JUST GROSS, MAN.
GROOOOAR
AND HE'S... SURPRISINGLY BRAVE.
ALSO, CAN WE TALK ABOUT THE STENCH? YOUR BREATH SMELLS LIKE TRASH JUICE ON A HOT DAY IN AUGUST.
WELL, THAT ONE'S TRUE.
SO LONG, STINKY!
WHOA! HE CAN EVEN JUMP LIKE ME!
BUT I'D COME UP WITH A BETTER INSULT THAN *STINKY*.

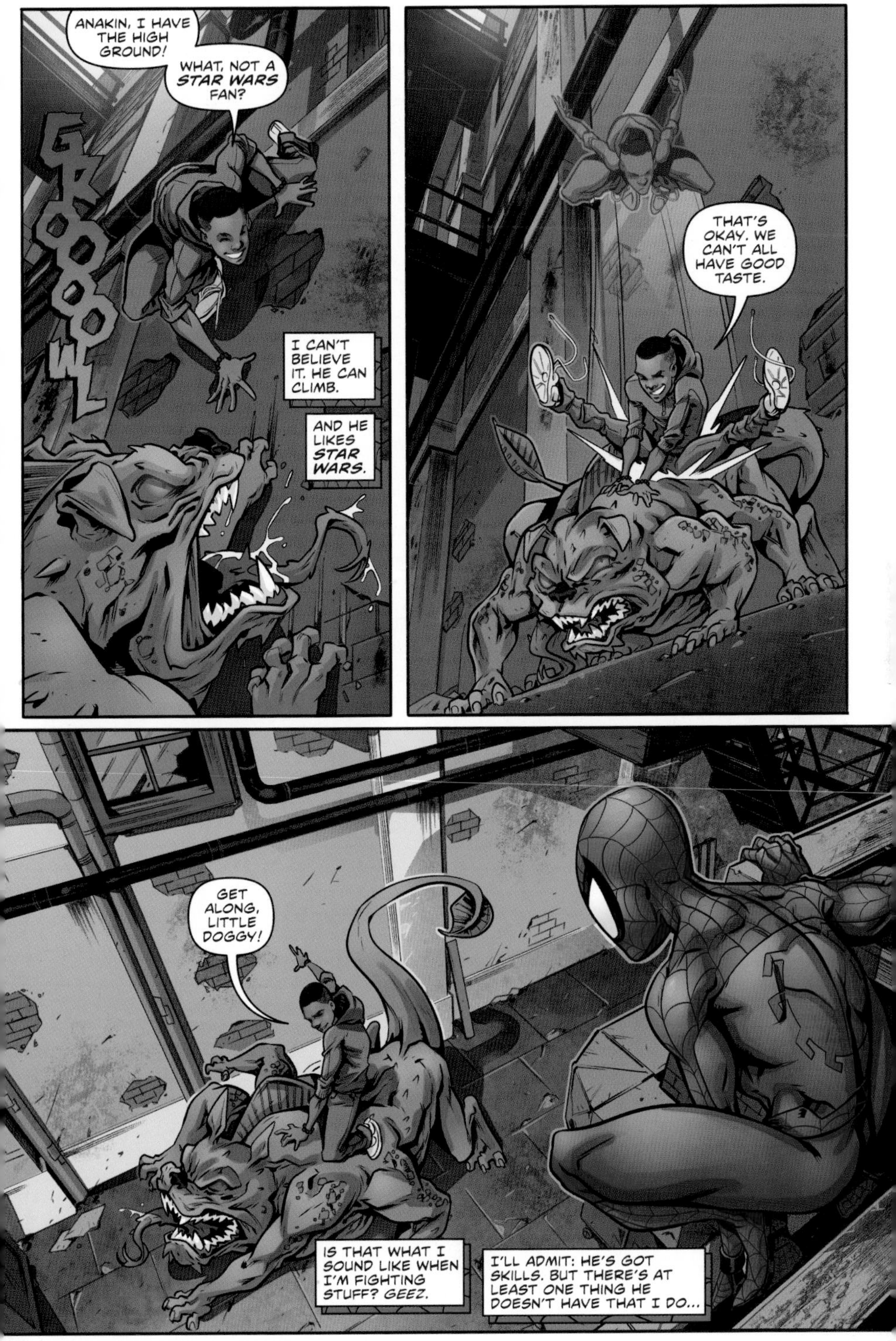
ANAKIN, I HAVE THE HIGH GROUND!
WHAT, NOT A STAR WARS FAN?
GROOOOOWL
I CAN'T BELIEVE IT. HE CAN CLIMB.
AND HE LIKES STAR WARS.
THAT'S OKAY. WE CAN'T ALL HAVE GOOD TASTE.
GET ALONG, LITTLE DOGGY!
IS THAT WHAT I SOUND LIKE WHEN I'M FIGHTING STUFF? GEEZ.
I'LL ADMIT: HE'S GOT SKILLS. BUT THERE'S AT LEAST ONE THING HE DOESN'T HAVE THAT I DO...

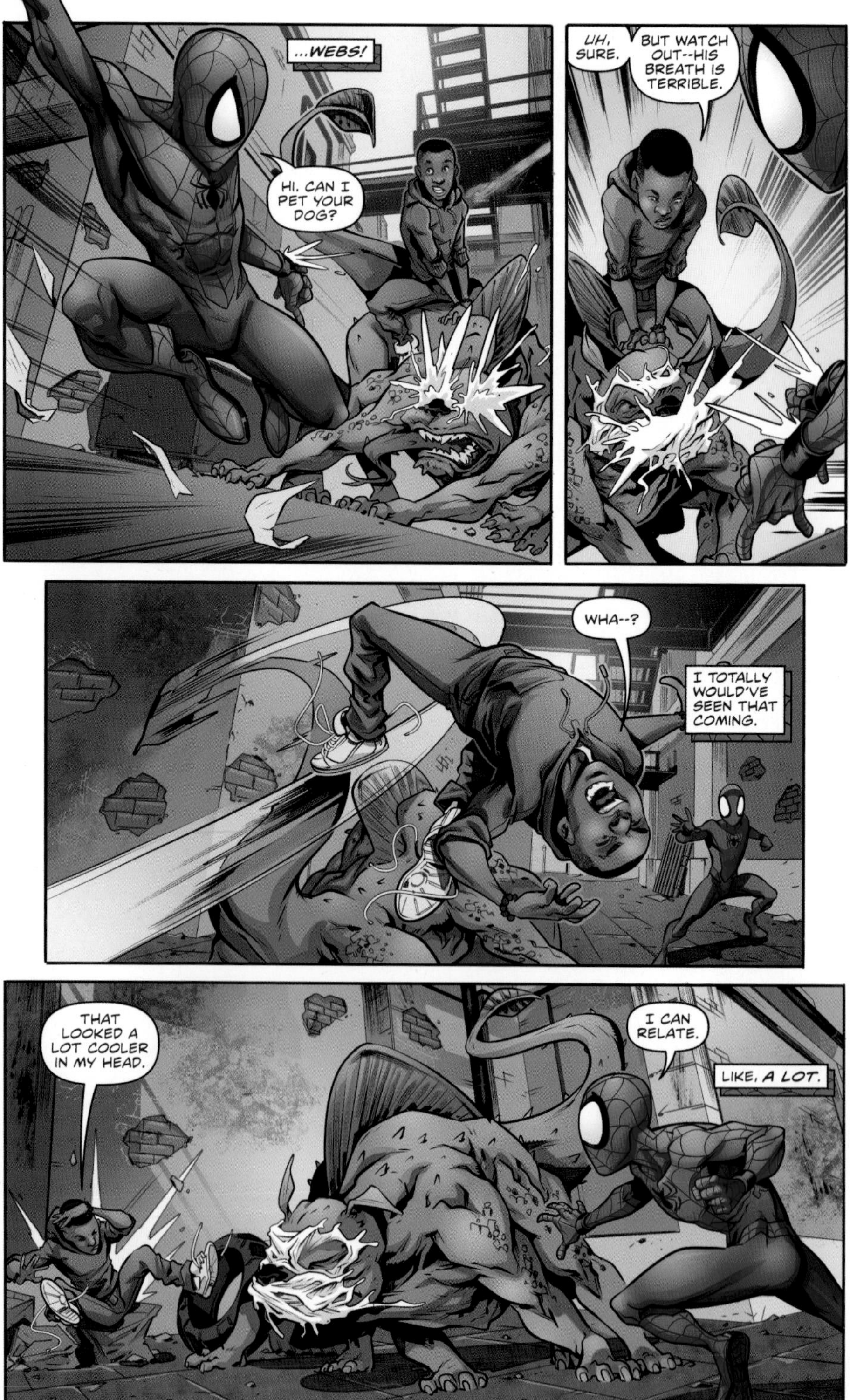
...WEBS!
HI. CAN I PET YOUR DOG?
UH, SURE.
BUT WATCH OUT--HIS BREATH IS TERRIBLE.
WHA--?
I TOTALLY WOULD'VE SEEN THAT COMING.
THAT LOOKED A LOT COOLER IN MY HEAD.
I CAN RELATE.
LIKE, A LOT.

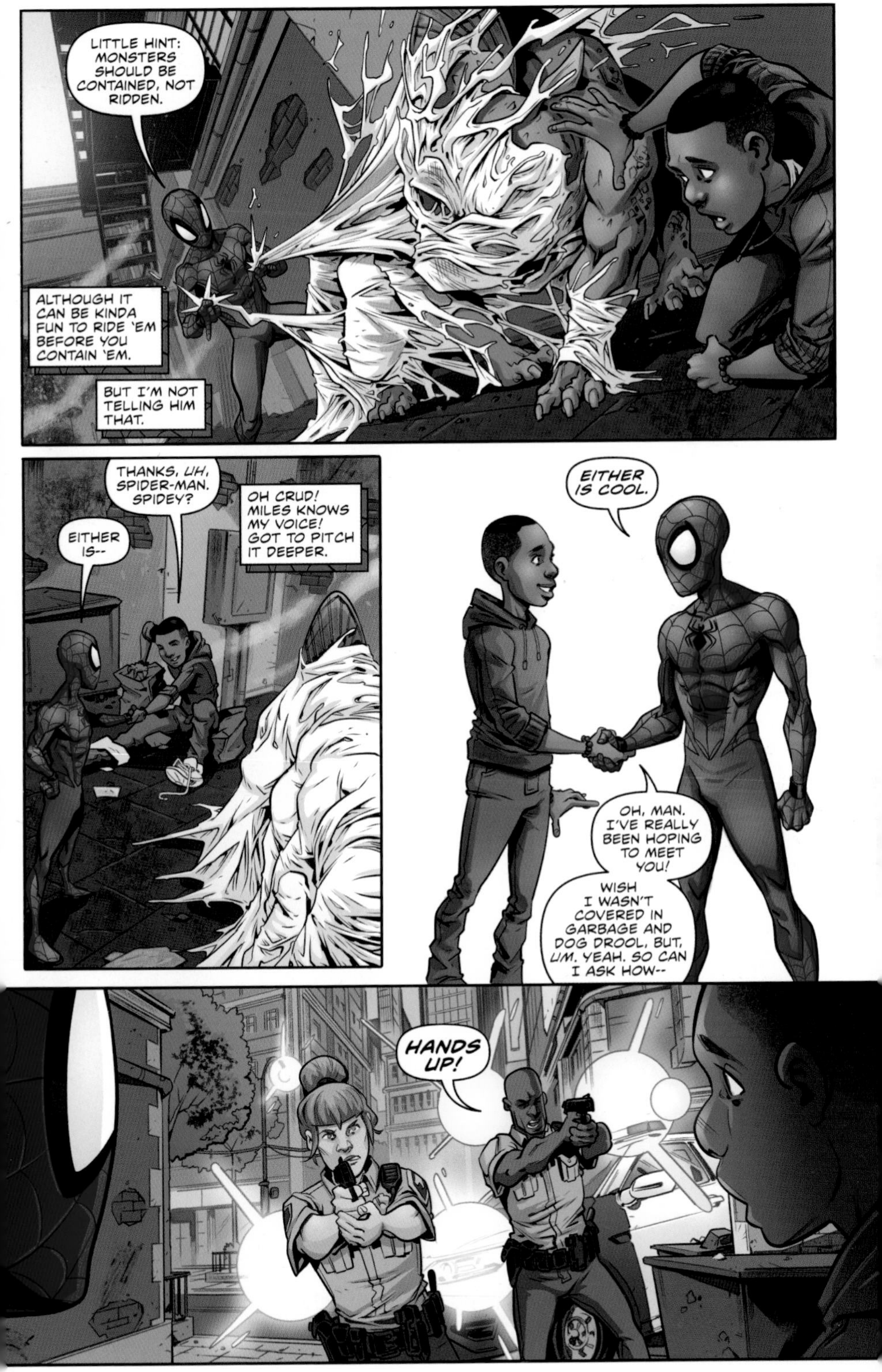
LITTLE HINT: MONSTERS SHOULD BE CONTAINED, NOT RIDDEN.
ALTHOUGH IT CAN BE KINDA FUN TO RIDE 'EM BEFORE YOU CONTAIN 'EM.
BUT I'M NOT TELLING HIM THAT.
THANKS, UH, SPIDER-MAN. SPIDEY?
EITHER IS--
OH CRUD! MILES KNOWS MY VOICE! GOT TO PITCH IT DEEPER.
EITHER IS COOL.
OH, MAN. I'VE REALLY BEEN HOPING TO MEET YOU!
WISH I WASN'T COVERED IN GARBAGE AND DOG DROOL, BUT, UM. YEAH. SO CAN I ASK HOW--
HANDS UP!

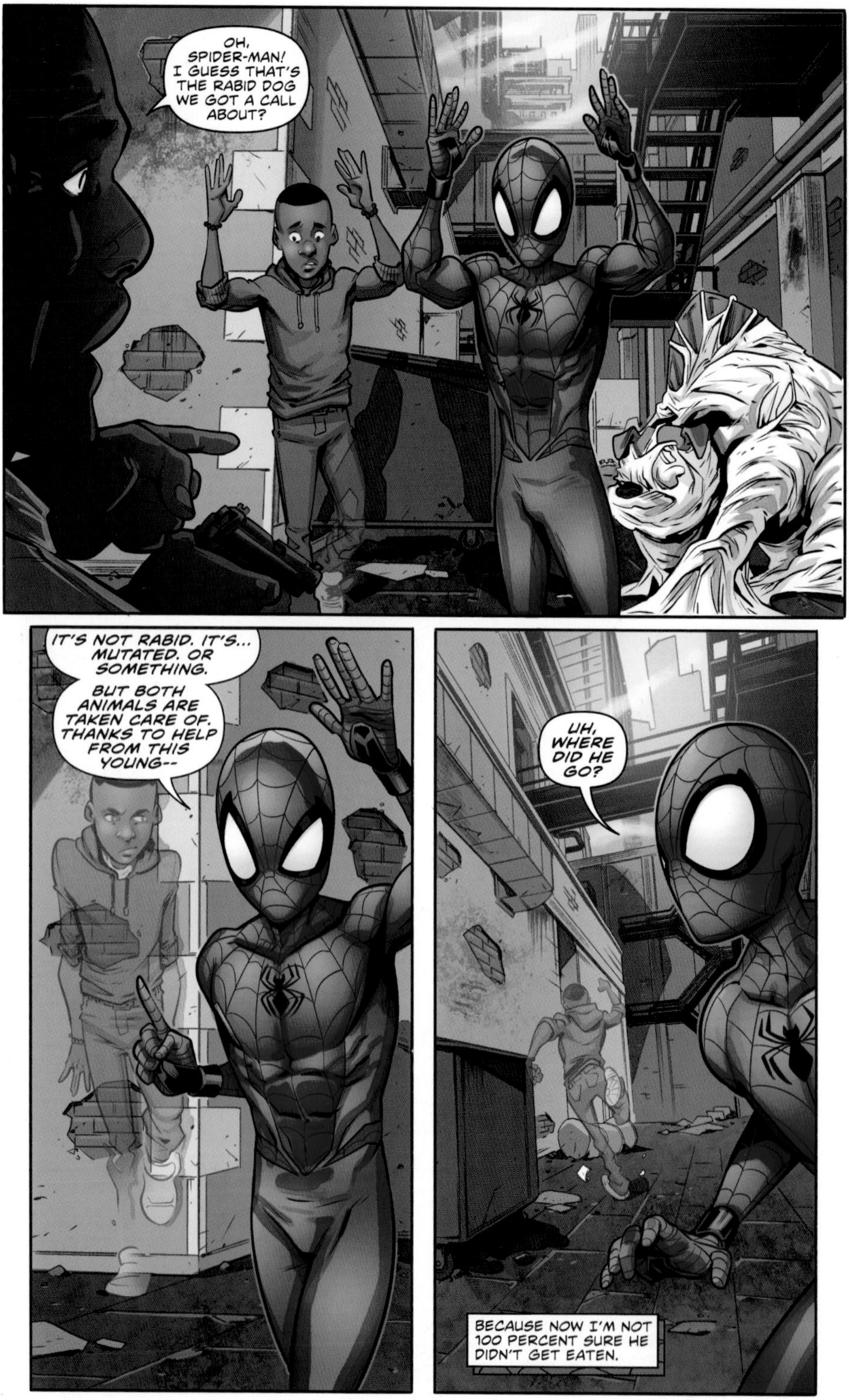
OH, SPIDER-MAN! I GUESS THAT'S THE RABID DOG WE GOT A CALL ABOUT?
IT'S NOT RABID. IT'S... MUTATED. OR SOMETHING.
BUT BOTH ANIMALS ARE TAKEN CARE OF. THANKS TO HELP FROM THIS YOUNG--
UH, WHERE DID HE GO?
BECAUSE NOW I'M NOT 100 PERCENT SURE HE DIDN'T GET EATEN.

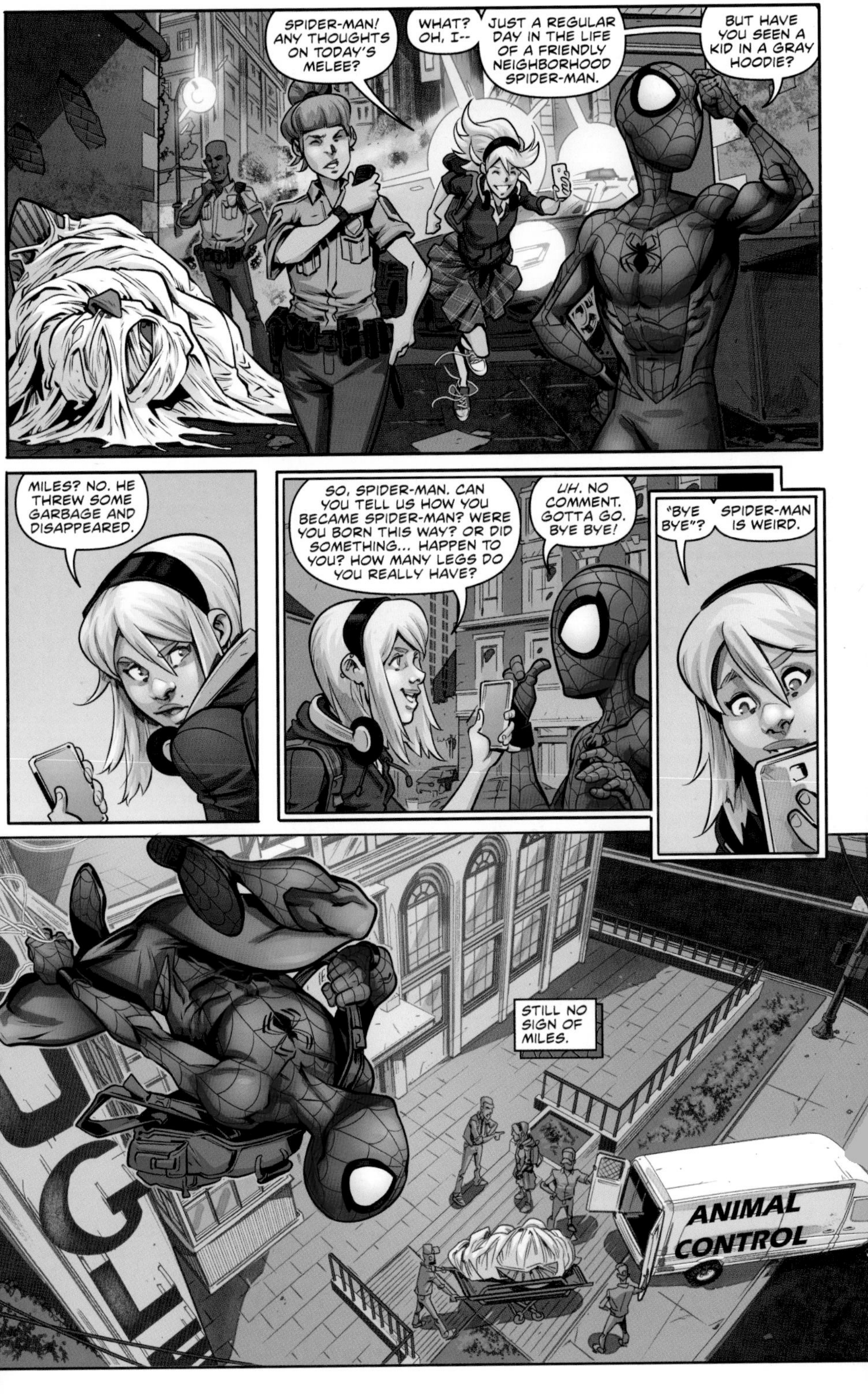

SPIDER-MAN! ANY THOUGHTS ON TODAY'S MELEE?
WHAT? OH, I--
JUST A REGULAR DAY IN THE LIFE OF A FRIENDLY NEIGHBORHOOD SPIDER-MAN.
BUT HAVE YOU SEEN A KID IN A GRAY HOODIE?
MILES? NO. HE THREW SOME GARBAGE AND DISAPPEARED.
SO, SPIDER-MAN. CAN YOU TELL US HOW YOU BECAME SPIDER-MAN? WERE YOU BORN THIS WAY? OR DID SOMETHING... HAPPEN TO YOU? HOW MANY LEGS DO YOU REALLY HAVE?
UH. NO COMMENT. GOTTA GO. BYE BYE!
"BYE BYE"?
SPIDER-MAN IS WEIRD.
STILL NO SIGN OF MILES.
ANIMAL CONTROL

SO MILES DISAPPEARED AND GWEN GETS CREDIT FOR THE STORY I STARRED IN. *AND* SHE KNOWS THE EDITOR. FANTASTIC.

I'VE GOT TO UP MY GAME.

DAILY BUGLE

SPIDER-MAN WRAPS UP RABID DOG

Photo by GWEN STACY

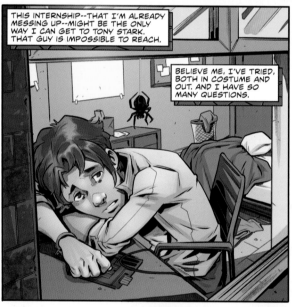

THIS INTERNSHIP--THAT I'M ALREADY MESSING UP--MIGHT BE THE ONLY WAY I CAN GET TO TONY STARK. THAT GUY IS IMPOSSIBLE TO REACH.

BELIEVE ME, I'VE TRIED, BOTH IN COSTUME AND OUT. AND I HAVE SO MANY QUESTIONS.

LIKE, HOW DID MILES DO... ALL THAT? HE CLIMBED THAT WALL. HE JUMPED SUPER HIGH. HE WAS CRAZY STRONG. I'VE NEVER SEEN ANYTHING LIKE IT.

EXCEPT...

...ME.

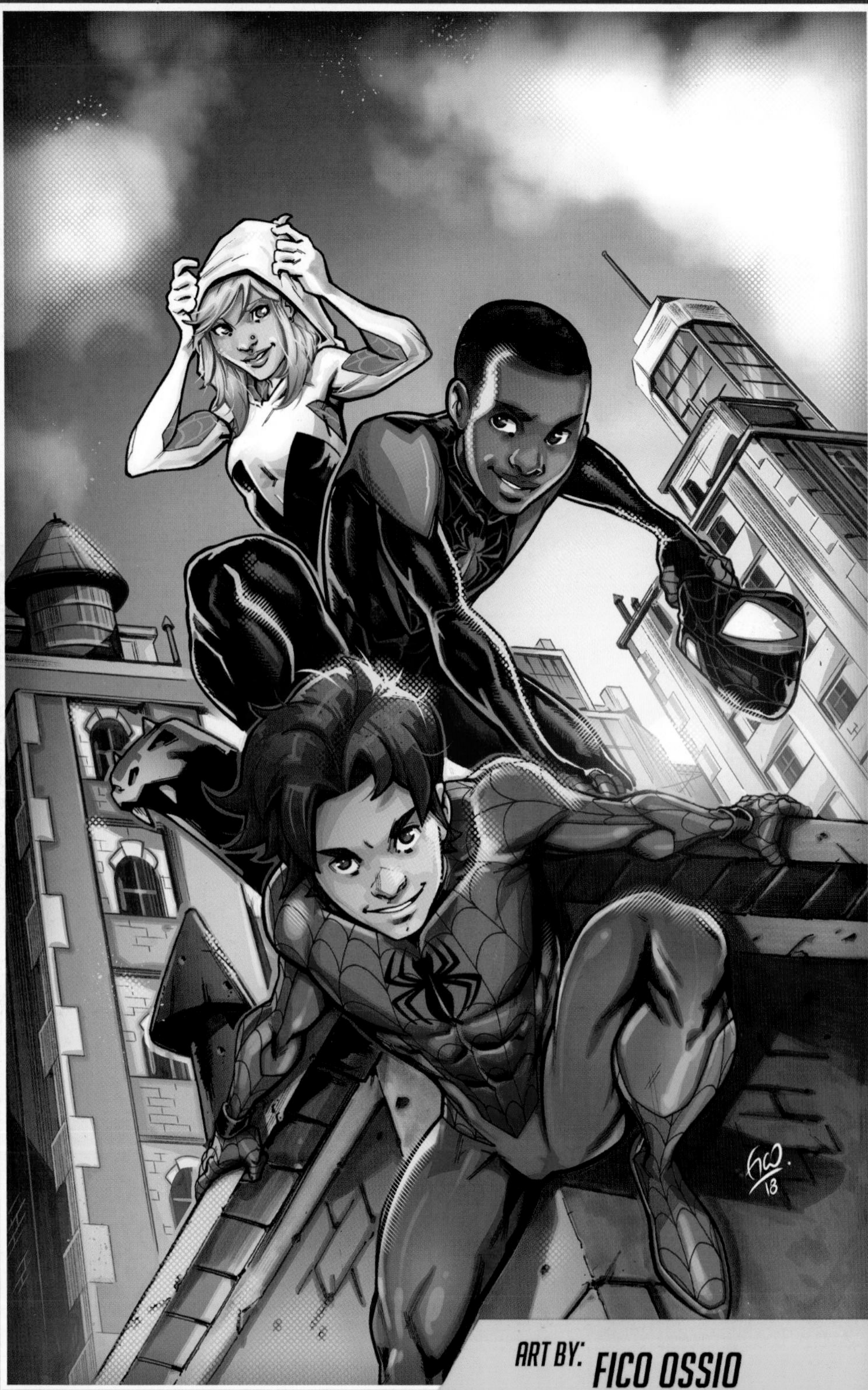

ART BY: FICO OSSIO

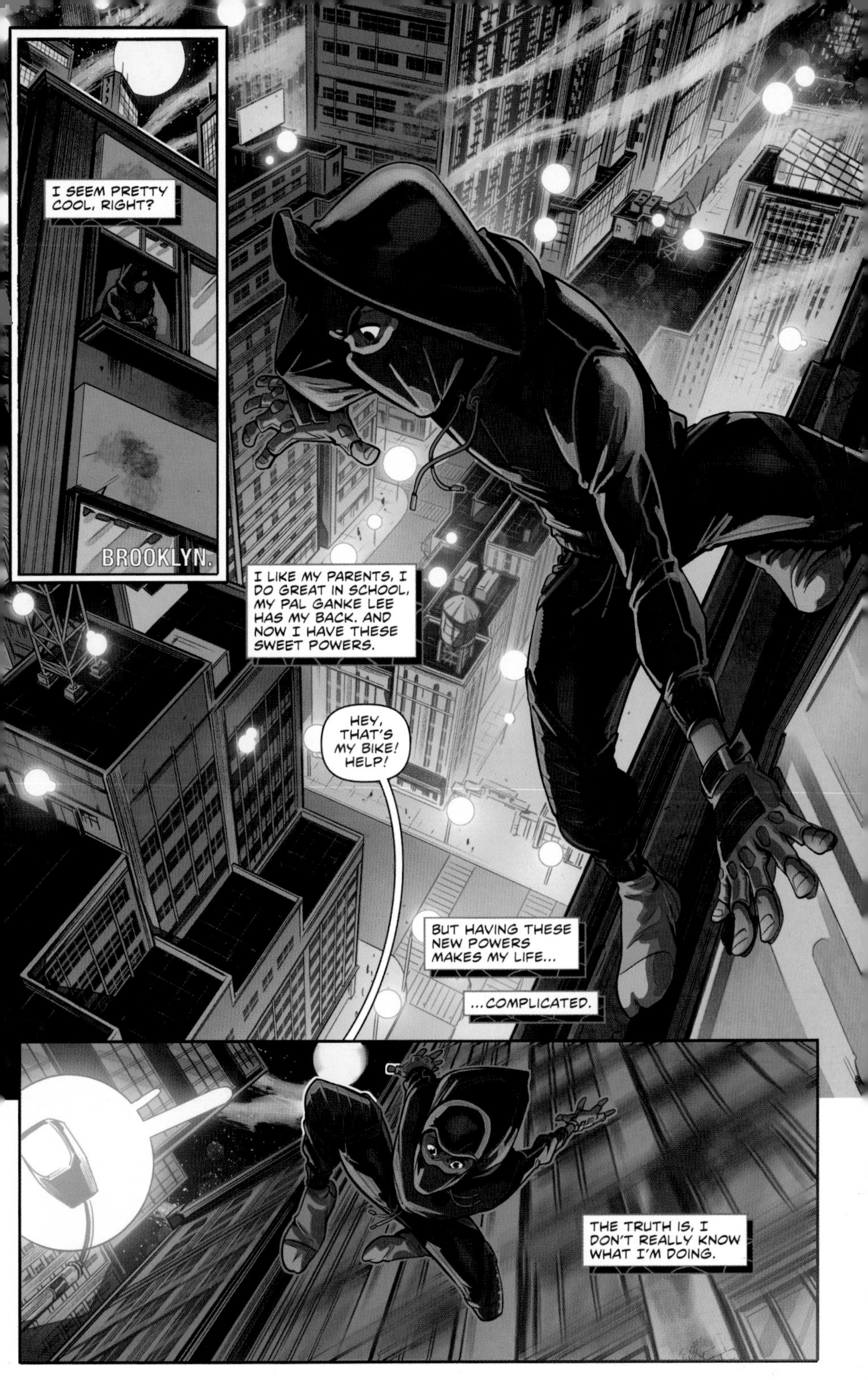
I SEEM PRETTY COOL, RIGHT?
BROOKLYN.
I LIKE MY PARENTS, I DO GREAT IN SCHOOL, MY PAL GANKE LEE HAS MY BACK. AND NOW I HAVE THESE SWEET POWERS.
HEY, THAT'S MY BIKE! HELP!
BUT HAVING THESE NEW POWERS MAKES MY LIFE...
...COMPLICATED.
THE TRUTH IS, I DON'T REALLY KNOW WHAT I'M DOING.

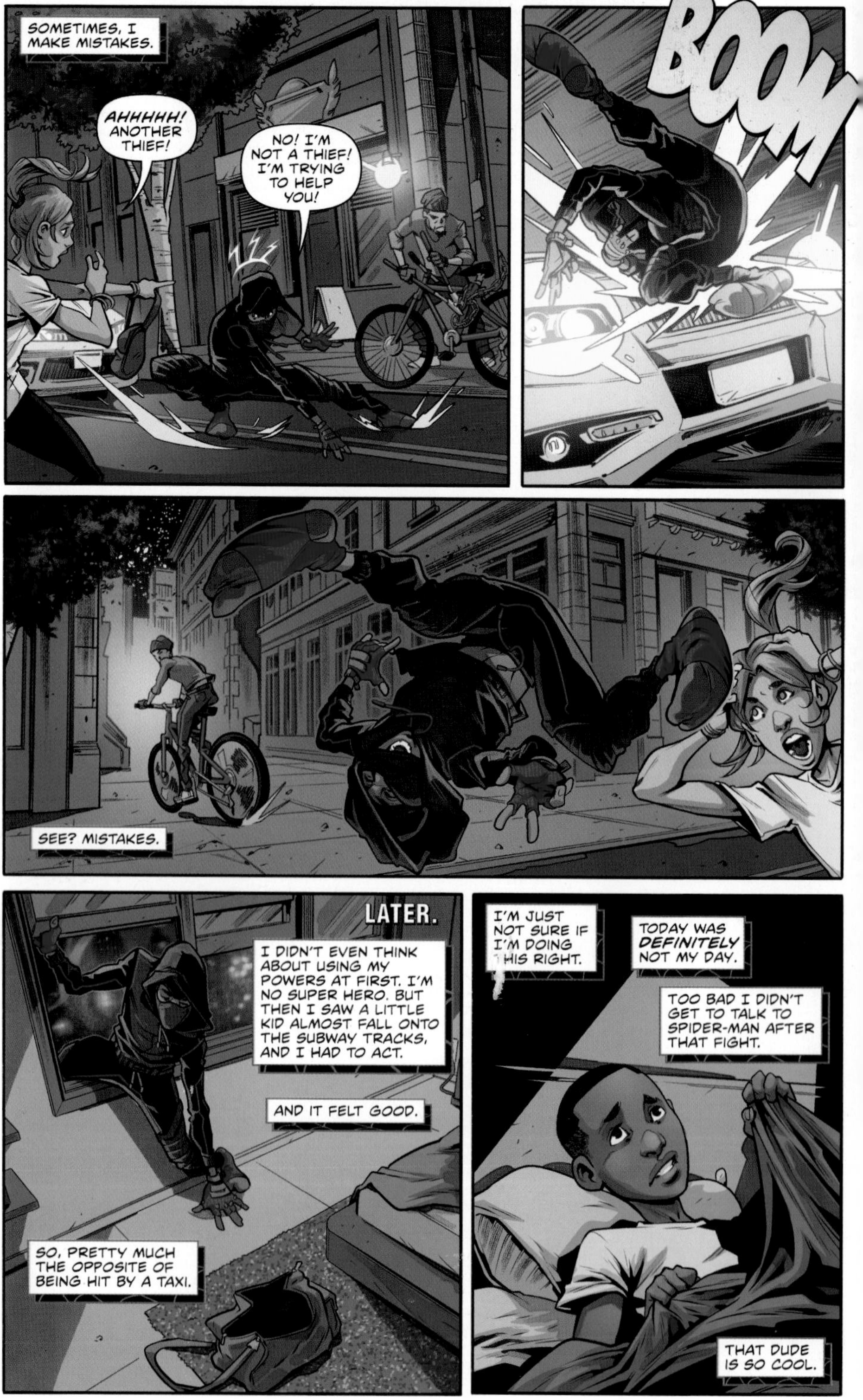
SOMETIMES, I MAKE MISTAKES.
AHHHHH! ANOTHER THIEF!
NO! I'M NOT A THIEF! I'M TRYING TO HELP YOU!
BOOM
SEE? MISTAKES.
LATER.
I DIDN'T EVEN THINK ABOUT USING MY POWERS AT FIRST. I'M NO SUPER HERO. BUT THEN I SAW A LITTLE KID ALMOST FALL ONTO THE SUBWAY TRACKS, AND I HAD TO ACT.
AND IT FELT GOOD.
SO, PRETTY MUCH THE OPPOSITE OF BEING HIT BY A TAXI.
I'M JUST NOT SURE IF I'M DOING THIS RIGHT.
TODAY WAS *DEFINITELY* NOT MY DAY.
TOO BAD I DIDN'T GET TO TALK TO SPIDER-MAN AFTER THAT FIGHT.
THAT DUDE IS SO COOL.

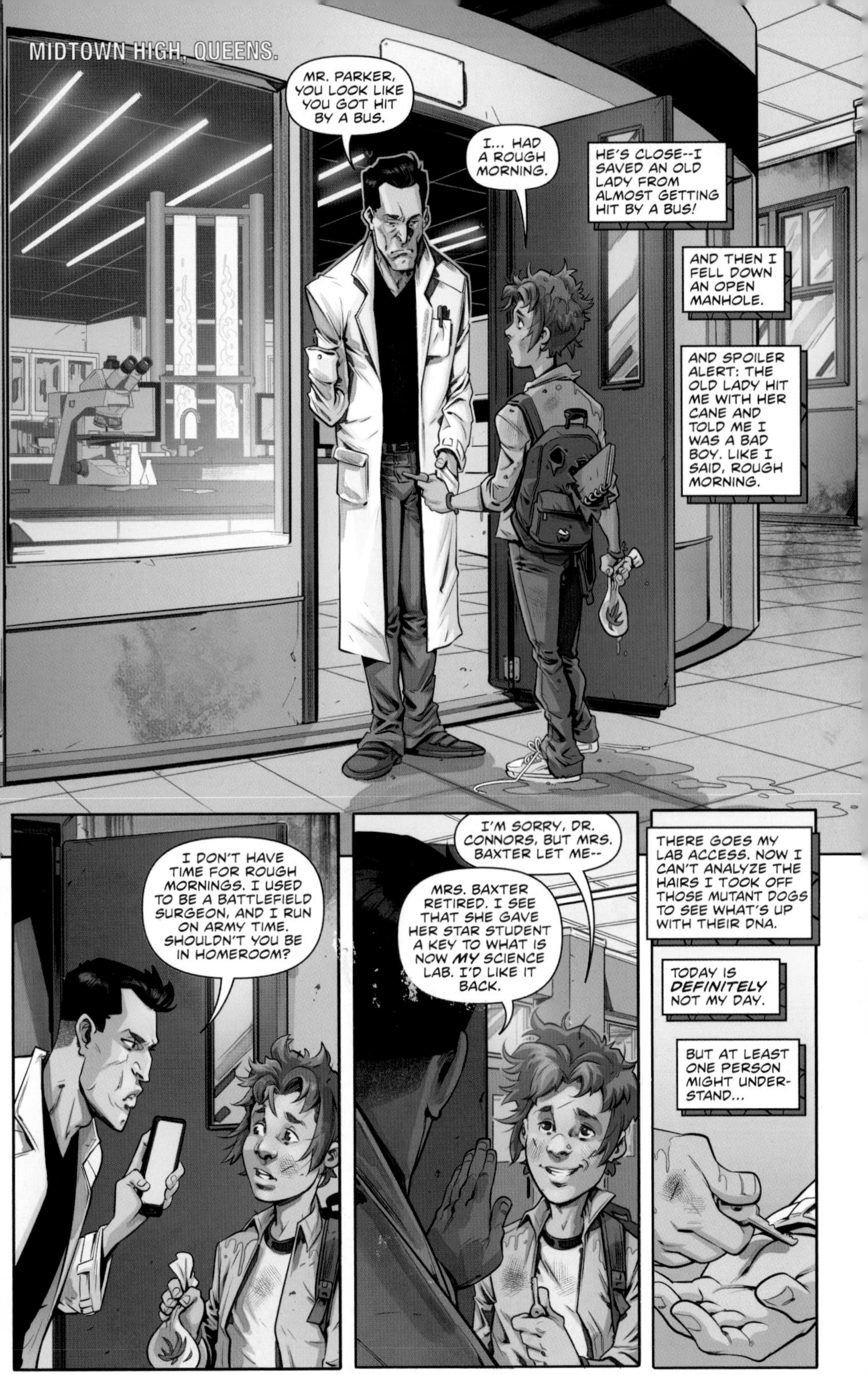

MIDTOWN HIGH, QUEENS.
MR. PARKER, YOU LOOK LIKE YOU GOT HIT BY A BUS.
I... HAD A ROUGH MORNING.
HE'S CLOSE--I SAVED AN OLD LADY FROM ALMOST GETTING HIT BY A BUS!
AND THEN I FELL DOWN AN OPEN MANHOLE.
AND SPOILER ALERT: THE OLD LADY HIT ME WITH HER CANE AND TOLD ME I WAS A BAD BOY. LIKE I SAID, ROUGH MORNING.
I DON'T HAVE TIME FOR ROUGH MORNINGS. I USED TO BE A BATTLEFIELD SURGEON, AND I RUN ON ARMY TIME. SHOULDN'T YOU BE IN HOMEROOM?
I'M SORRY, DR. CONNORS, BUT MRS. BAXTER LET ME--
MRS. BAXTER RETIRED. I SEE THAT SHE GAVE HER STAR STUDENT A KEY TO WHAT IS NOW *MY* SCIENCE LAB. I'D LIKE IT BACK.
THERE GOES MY LAB ACCESS. NOW I CAN'T ANALYZE THE HAIRS I TOOK OFF THOSE MUTANT DOGS TO SEE WHAT'S UP WITH THEIR DNA.
TODAY IS ***DEFINITELY*** NOT MY DAY.
BUT AT LEAST ONE PERSON MIGHT UNDER-STAND...

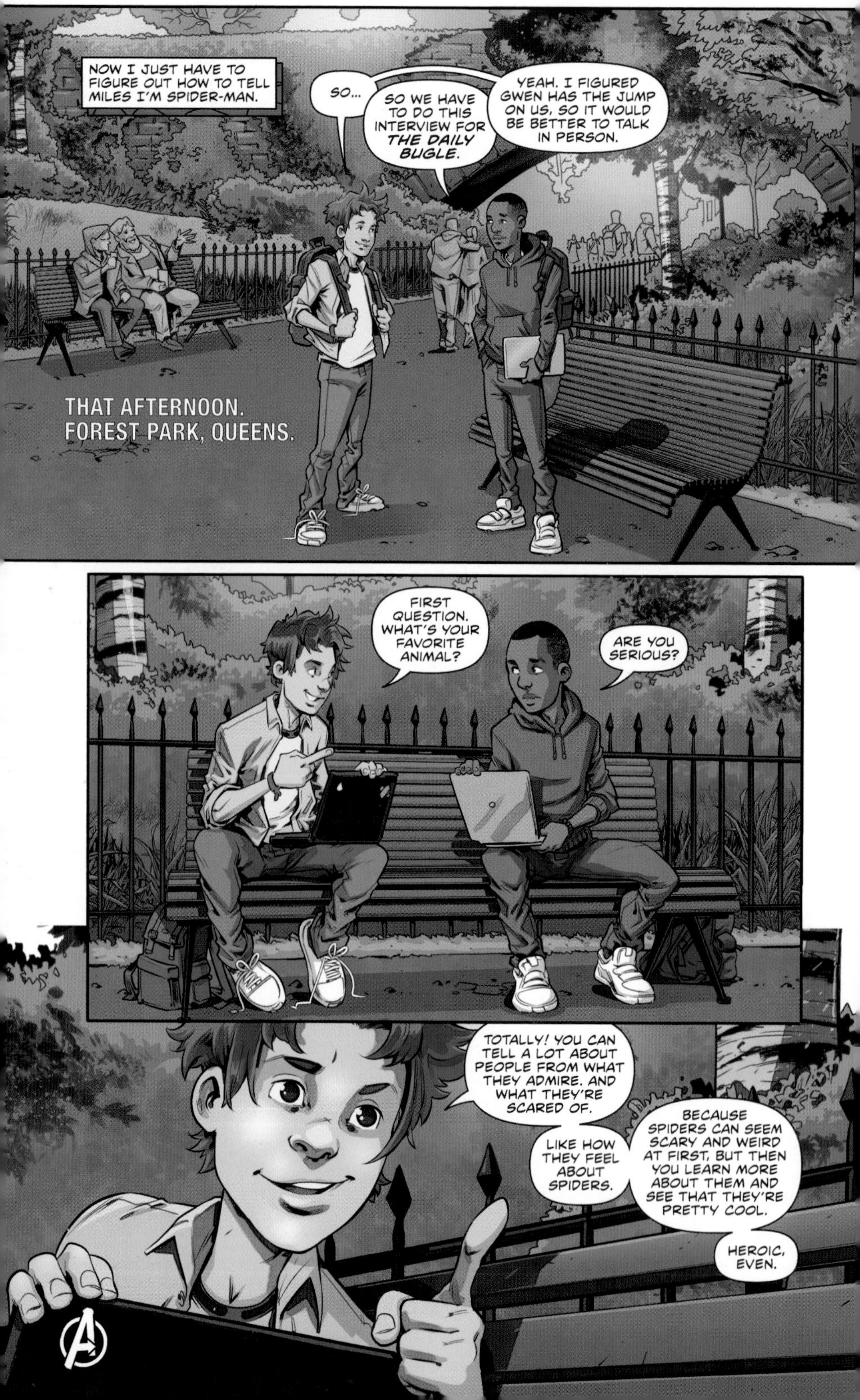
NOW I JUST HAVE TO FIGURE OUT HOW TO TELL MILES I'M SPIDER-MAN.
SO...
SO WE HAVE TO DO THIS INTERVIEW FOR *THE DAILY BUGLE*.
YEAH. I FIGURED GWEN HAS THE JUMP ON US, SO IT WOULD BE BETTER TO TALK IN PERSON.
THAT AFTERNOON. FOREST PARK, QUEENS.
FIRST QUESTION. WHAT'S YOUR FAVORITE ANIMAL?
ARE YOU SERIOUS?
TOTALLY! YOU CAN TELL A LOT ABOUT PEOPLE FROM WHAT THEY ADMIRE. AND WHAT THEY'RE SCARED OF.
LIKE HOW THEY FEEL ABOUT SPIDERS.
BECAUSE SPIDERS CAN SEEM SCARY AND WEIRD AT FIRST, BUT THEN YOU LEARN MORE ABOUT THEM AND SEE THAT THEY'RE PRETTY COOL.
HEROIC, EVEN.

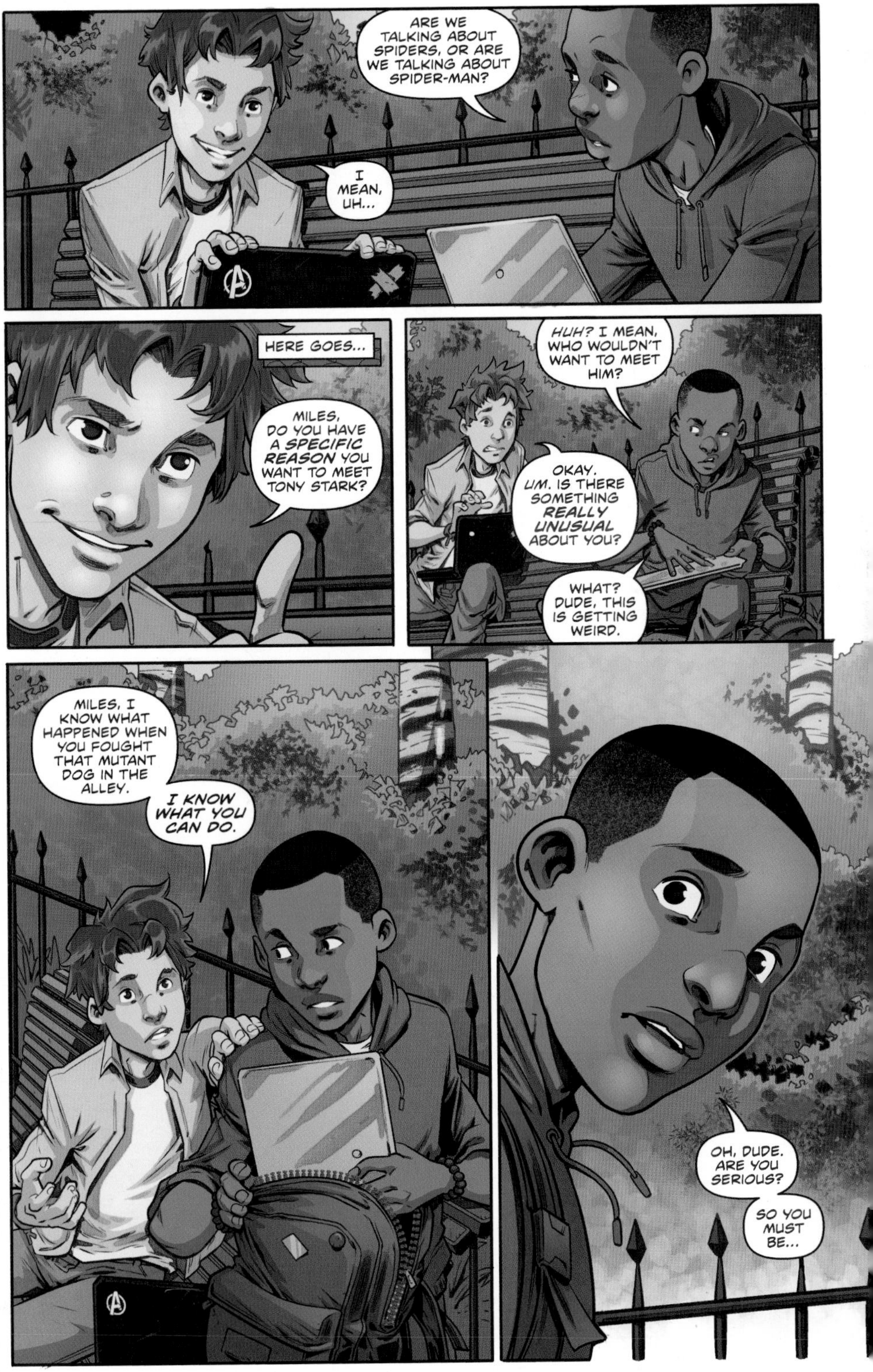
ARE WE TALKING ABOUT SPIDERS, OR ARE WE TALKING ABOUT SPIDER-MAN?
I MEAN, UH...
HERE GOES...
MILES, DO YOU HAVE A SPECIFIC REASON YOU WANT TO MEET TONY STARK?
HUH? I MEAN, WHO WOULDN'T WANT TO MEET HIM?
OKAY. UM. IS THERE SOMETHING REALLY UNUSUAL ABOUT YOU?
WHAT? DUDE, THIS IS GETTING WEIRD.
MILES, I KNOW WHAT HAPPENED WHEN YOU FOUGHT THAT MUTANT DOG IN THE ALLEY.
I KNOW WHAT YOU CAN DO.
OH, DUDE. ARE YOU SERIOUS?
SO YOU MUST BE...

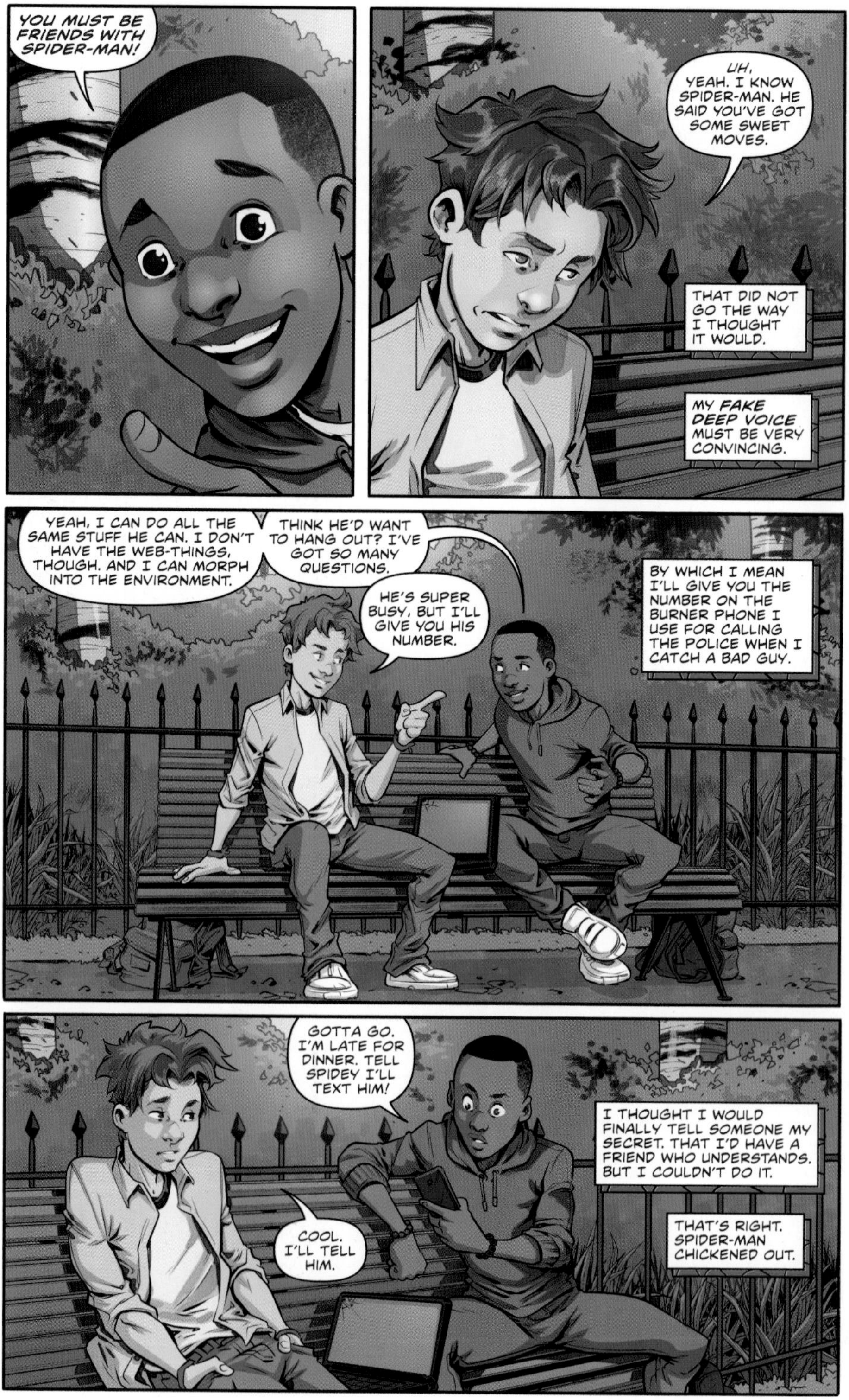
YOU MUST BE FRIENDS WITH SPIDER-MAN!
UH, YEAH. I KNOW SPIDER-MAN. HE SAID YOU'VE GOT SOME SWEET MOVES.
THAT DID NOT GO THE WAY I THOUGHT IT WOULD.
MY FAKE DEEP VOICE MUST BE VERY CONVINCING.
YEAH, I CAN DO ALL THE SAME STUFF HE CAN. I DON'T HAVE THE WEB-THINGS, THOUGH. AND I CAN MORPH INTO THE ENVIRONMENT.
THINK HE'D WANT TO HANG OUT? I'VE GOT SO MANY QUESTIONS.
HE'S SUPER BUSY, BUT I'LL GIVE YOU HIS NUMBER.
BY WHICH I MEAN I'LL GIVE YOU THE NUMBER ON THE BURNER PHONE I USE FOR CALLING THE POLICE WHEN I CATCH A BAD GUY.
GOTTA GO. I'M LATE FOR DINNER. TELL SPIDEY I'LL TEXT HIM!
COOL. I'LL TELL HIM.
I THOUGHT I WOULD FINALLY TELL SOMEONE MY SECRET. THAT I'D HAVE A FRIEND WHO UNDERSTANDS. BUT I COULDN'T DO IT.
THAT'S RIGHT. SPIDER-MAN CHICKENED OUT.

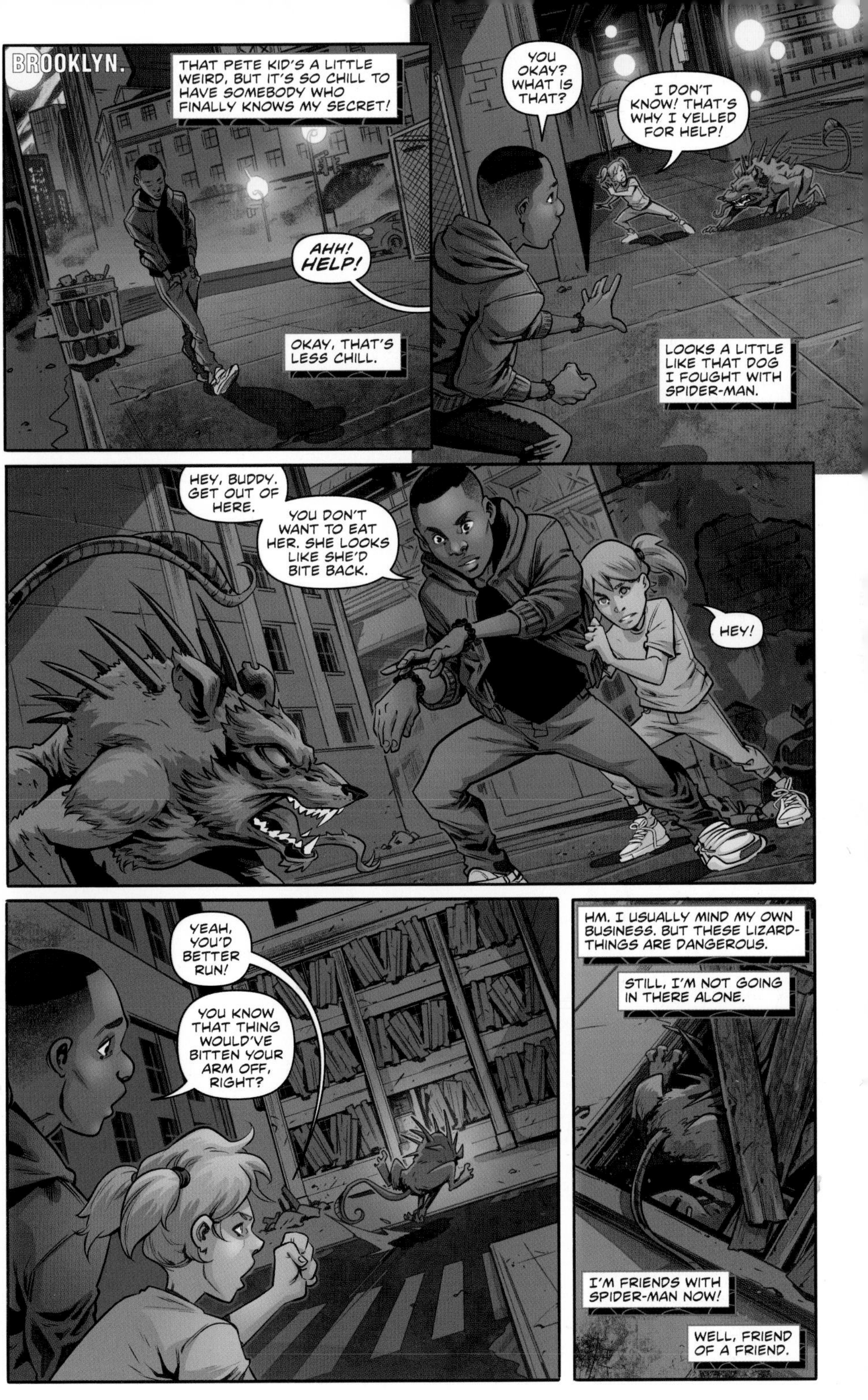
BROOKLYN.
THAT PETE KID'S A LITTLE WEIRD, BUT IT'S SO CHILL TO HAVE SOMEBODY WHO FINALLY KNOWS MY SECRET!
AHH! HELP!
OKAY, THAT'S LESS CHILL.
YOU OKAY? WHAT IS THAT?
I DON'T KNOW! THAT'S WHY I YELLED FOR HELP!
LOOKS A LITTLE LIKE THAT DOG I FOUGHT WITH SPIDER-MAN.
HEY, BUDDY. GET OUT OF HERE.
YOU DON'T WANT TO EAT HER. SHE LOOKS LIKE SHE'D BITE BACK.
HEY!
YEAH, YOU'D BETTER RUN!
YOU KNOW THAT THING WOULD'VE BITTEN YOUR ARM OFF, RIGHT?
HM. I USUALLY MIND MY OWN BUSINESS. BUT THESE LIZARD-THINGS ARE DANGEROUS.
STILL, I'M NOT GOING IN THERE ALONE.
I'M FRIENDS WITH SPIDER-MAN NOW!
WELL, FRIEND OF A FRIEND.

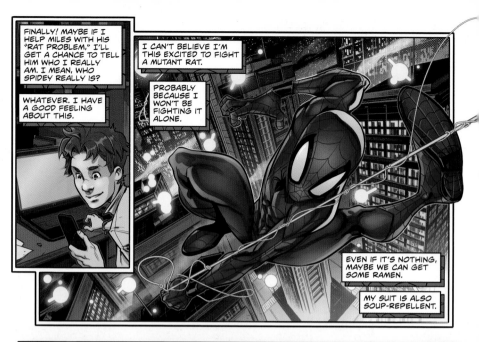

FINALLY! MAYBE IF I HELP MILES WITH HIS "RAT PROBLEM," I'LL GET A CHANCE TO TELL HIM WHO I REALLY AM. I MEAN, WHO SPIDEY REALLY IS?

WHATEVER. I HAVE A GOOD FEELING ABOUT THIS.

I CAN'T BELIEVE I'M THIS EXCITED TO FIGHT A MUTANT RAT.

PROBABLY BECAUSE I WON'T BE FIGHTING IT ALONE.

EVEN IF IT'S NOTHING, MAYBE WE CAN GET SOME RAMEN.

MY SUIT IS ALSO SOUP-REPELLENT.

HI. MILES?

YEAH. HI.

NO MORE *FAKE DEEP VOICE.* NOW I *WANT* HIM TO GUESS.

UH, HAS ANYONE EVER TOLD YOU THAT YOU LOOK LIKE A BURGLAR?

EVERY TIME I WEAR THIS. THAT'S PROBABLY NOT A GOOD SIGN.

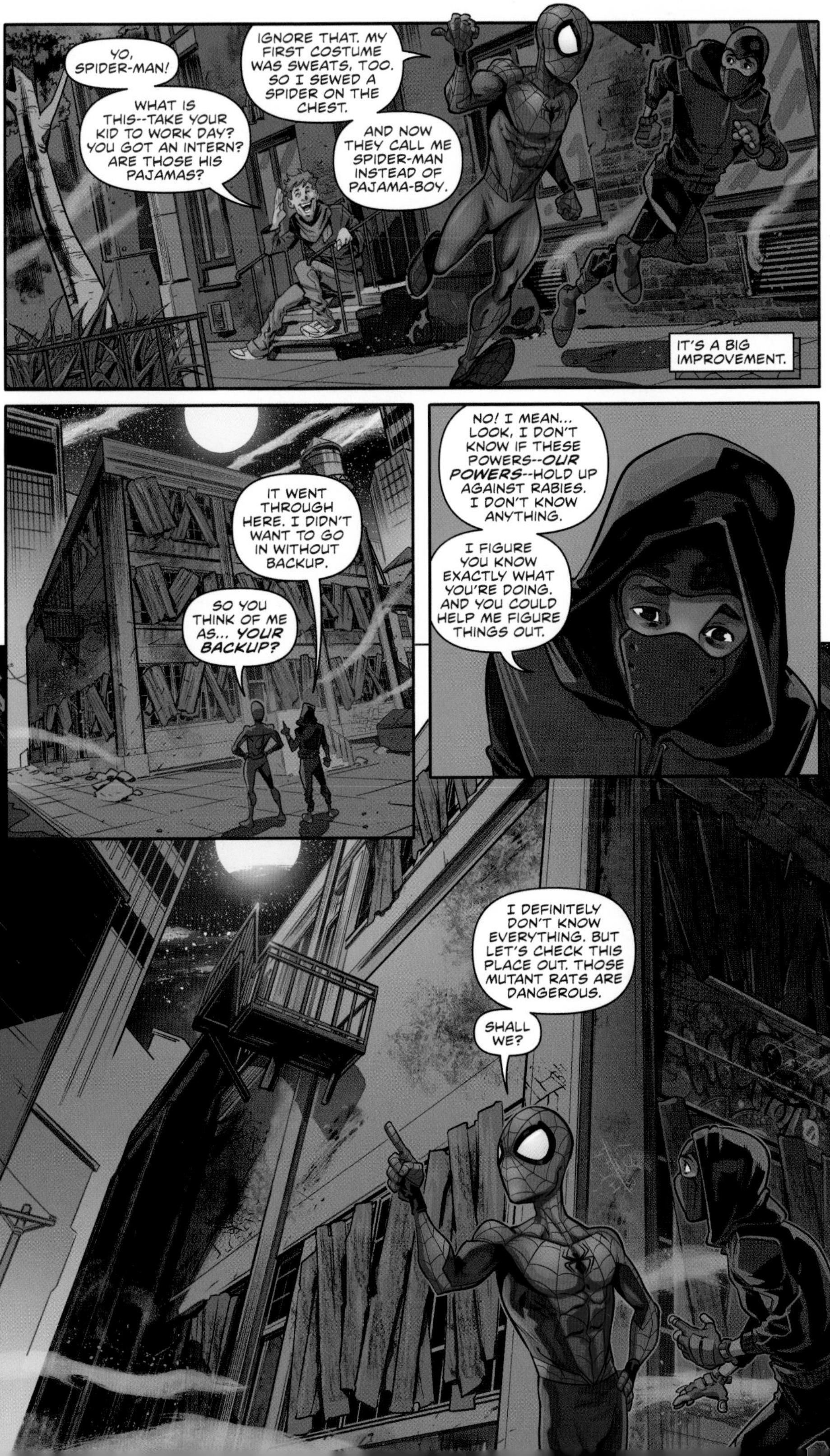
YO, SPIDER-MAN!
WHAT IS THIS--TAKE YOUR KID TO WORK DAY? YOU GOT AN INTERN? ARE THOSE HIS PAJAMAS?
IGNORE THAT. MY FIRST COSTUME WAS SWEATS, TOO. SO I SEWED A SPIDER ON THE CHEST.
AND NOW THEY CALL ME SPIDER-MAN INSTEAD OF PAJAMA-BOY.
IT'S A BIG IMPROVEMENT.
IT WENT THROUGH HERE. I DIDN'T WANT TO GO IN WITHOUT BACKUP.
SO YOU THINK OF ME AS... YOUR BACKUP?
NO! I MEAN... LOOK, I DON'T KNOW IF THESE POWERS--OUR POWERS--HOLD UP AGAINST RABIES. I DON'T KNOW ANYTHING.
I FIGURE YOU KNOW EXACTLY WHAT YOU'RE DOING. AND YOU COULD HELP ME FIGURE THINGS OUT.
I DEFINITELY DON'T KNOW EVERYTHING. BUT LET'S CHECK THIS PLACE OUT. THOSE MUTANT RATS ARE DANGEROUS.
SHALL WE?

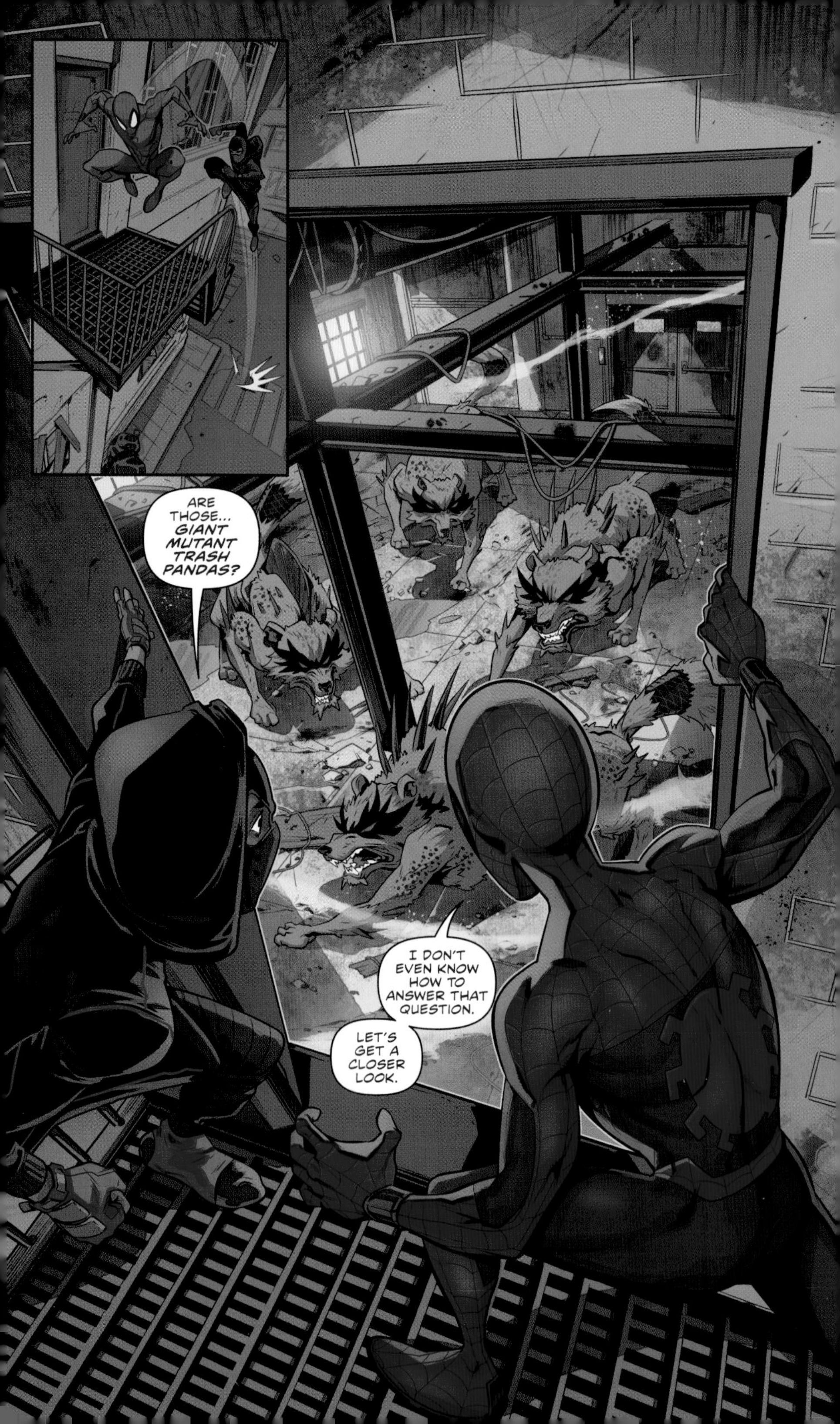
ARE THOSE... GIANT MUTANT TRASH PANDAS?
I DON'T EVEN KNOW HOW TO ANSWER THAT QUESTION.
LET'S GET A CLOSER LOOK.

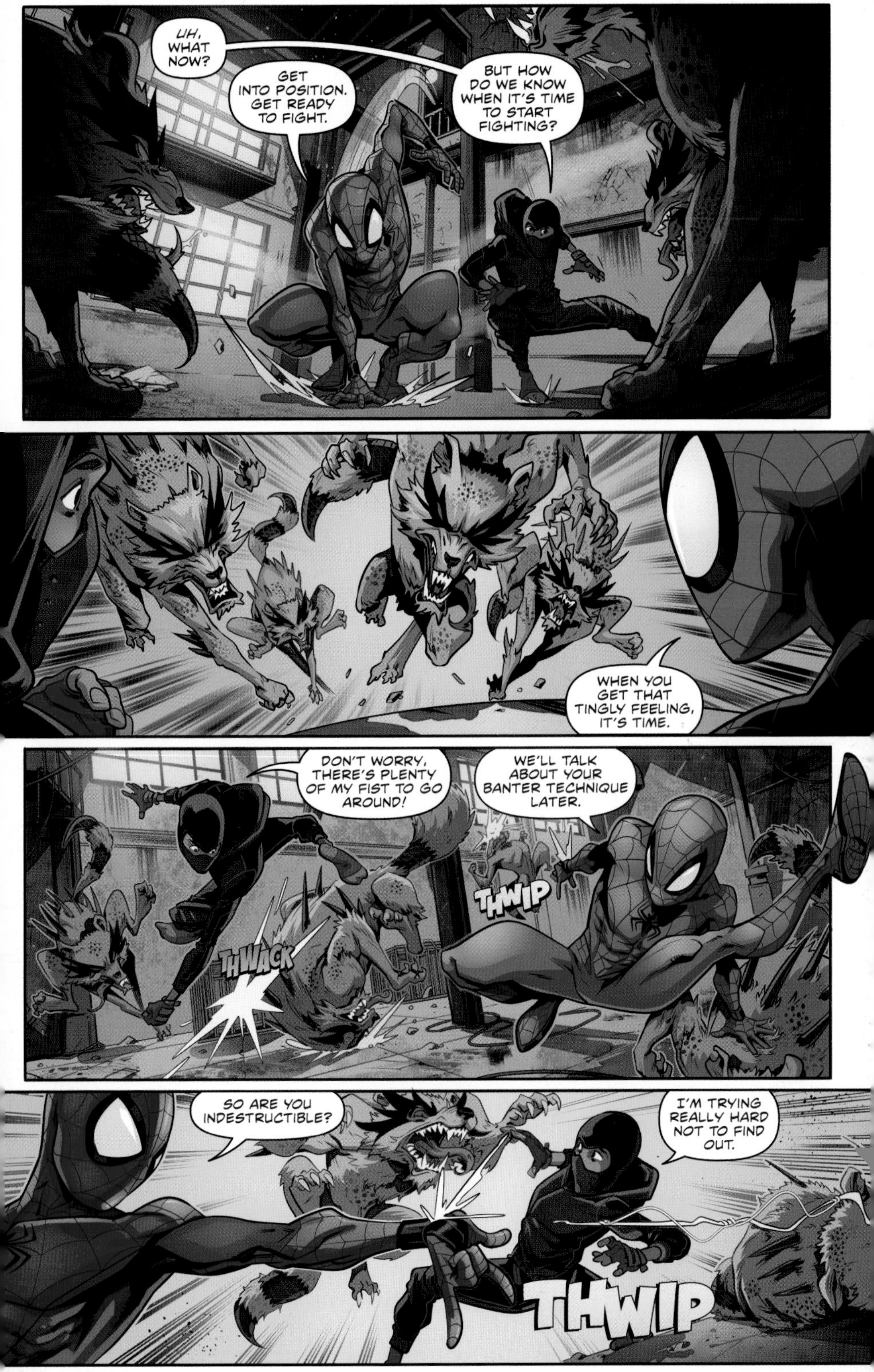

UH, WHAT NOW?
GET INTO POSITION. GET READY TO FIGHT.
BUT HOW DO WE KNOW WHEN IT'S TIME TO START FIGHTING?
WHEN YOU GET THAT TINGLY FEELING, IT'S TIME.
DON'T WORRY, THERE'S PLENTY OF MY FIST TO GO AROUND!
WE'LL TALK ABOUT YOUR BANTER TECHNIQUE LATER.
THWIP
THWACK
SO ARE YOU INDESTRUCTIBLE?
I'M TRYING REALLY HARD NOT TO FIND OUT.
THWIP

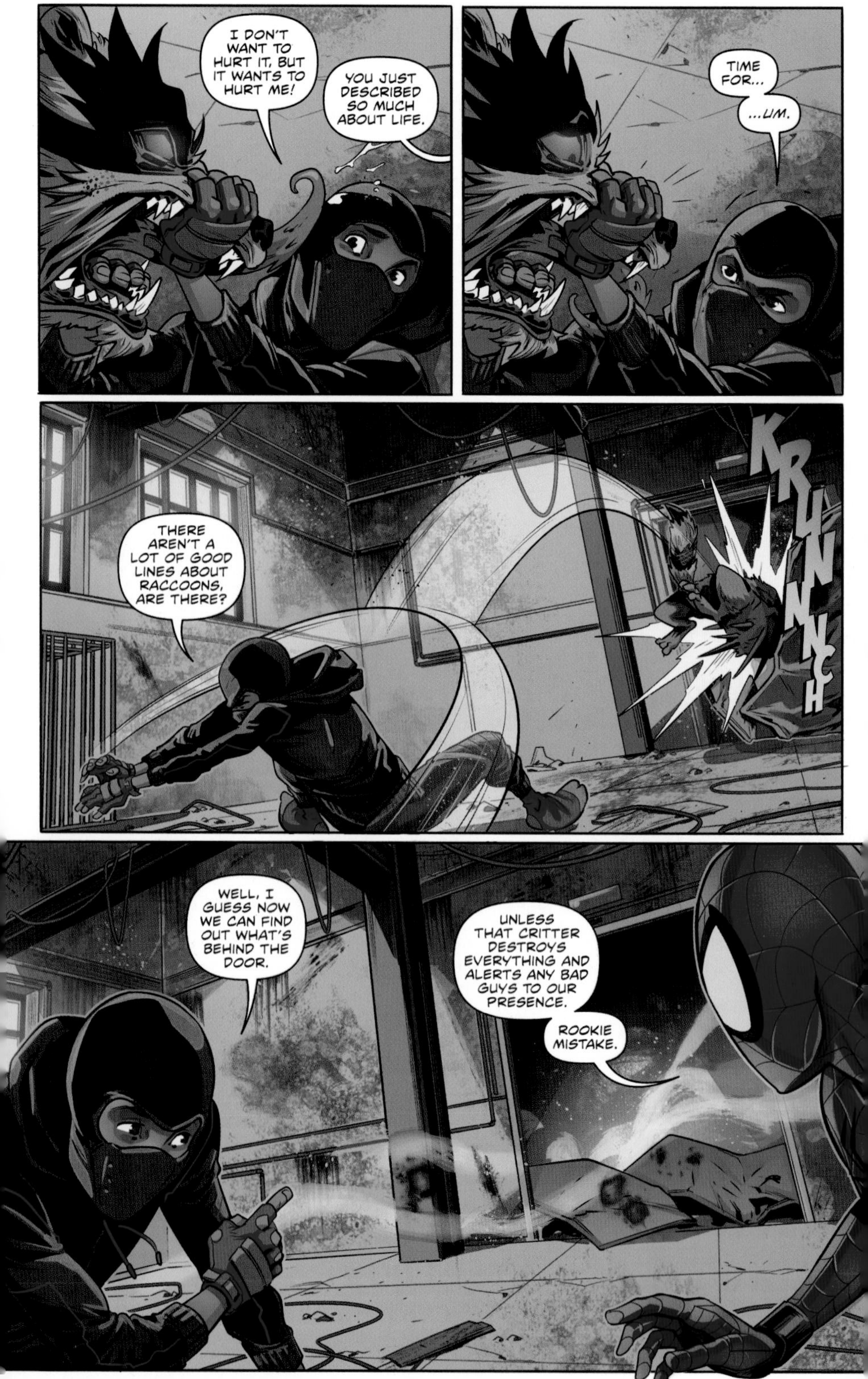
I DON'T WANT TO HURT IT, BUT IT WANTS TO HURT ME!
YOU JUST DESCRIBED SO MUCH ABOUT LIFE.
TIME FOR...
...UM.
THERE AREN'T A LOT OF GOOD LINES ABOUT RACCOONS, ARE THERE?
KRUNNNCH
WELL, I GUESS NOW WE CAN FIND OUT WHAT'S BEHIND THE DOOR.
UNLESS THAT CRITTER DESTROYS EVERYTHING AND ALERTS ANY BAD GUYS TO OUR PRESENCE.
ROOKIE MISTAKE.

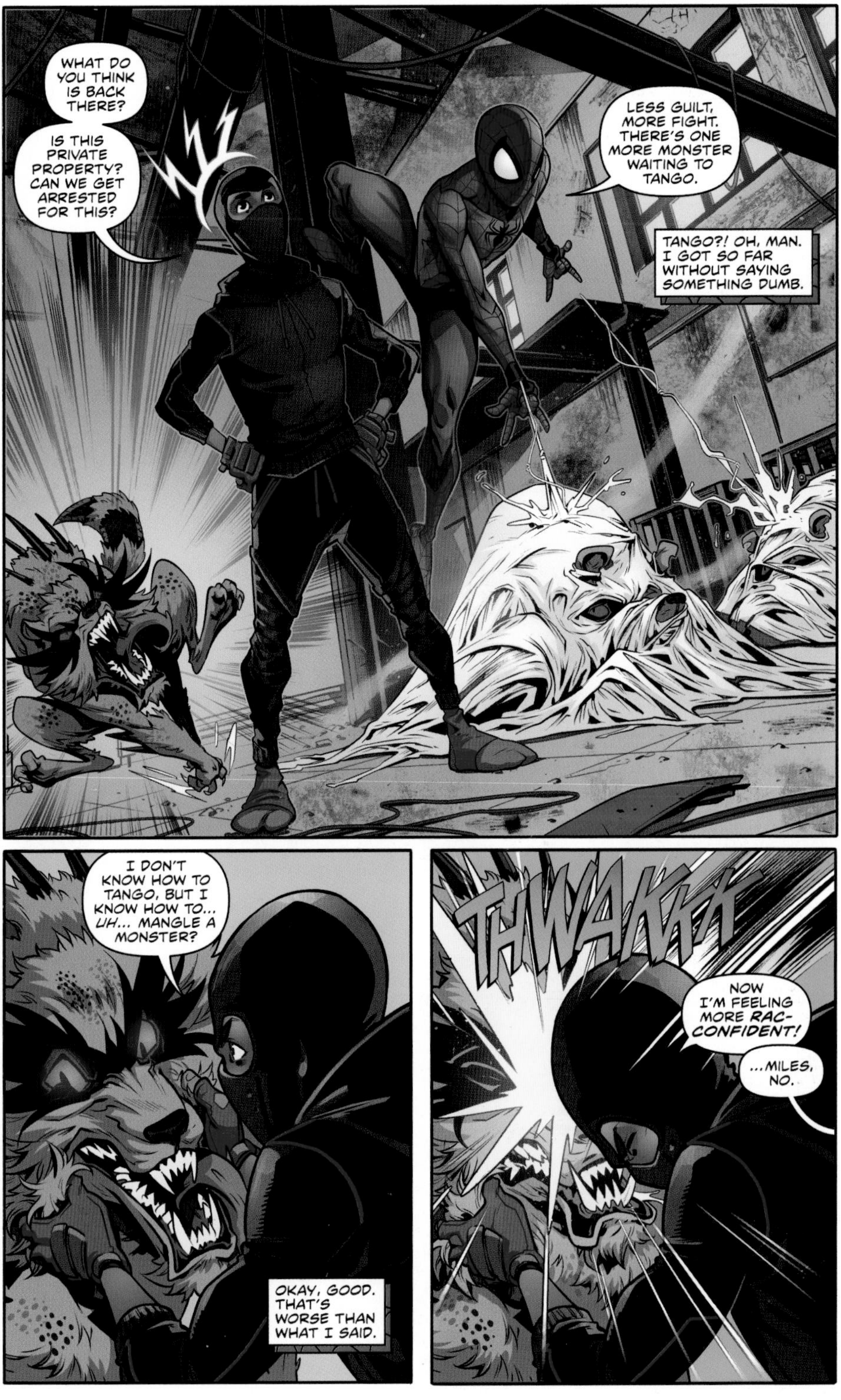
WHAT DO YOU THINK IS BACK THERE?
IS THIS PRIVATE PROPERTY? CAN WE GET ARRESTED FOR THIS?
LESS GUILT, MORE FIGHT. THERE'S ONE MORE MONSTER WAITING TO TANGO.
TANGO?! OH, MAN. I GOT SO FAR WITHOUT SAYING SOMETHING DUMB.
I DON'T KNOW HOW TO TANGO, BUT I KNOW HOW TO... UH... MANGLE A MONSTER?
OKAY, GOOD. THAT'S WORSE THAN WHAT I SAID.
THWAKKK
NOW I'M FEELING MORE RAC-CONFIDENT!
...MILES, NO.

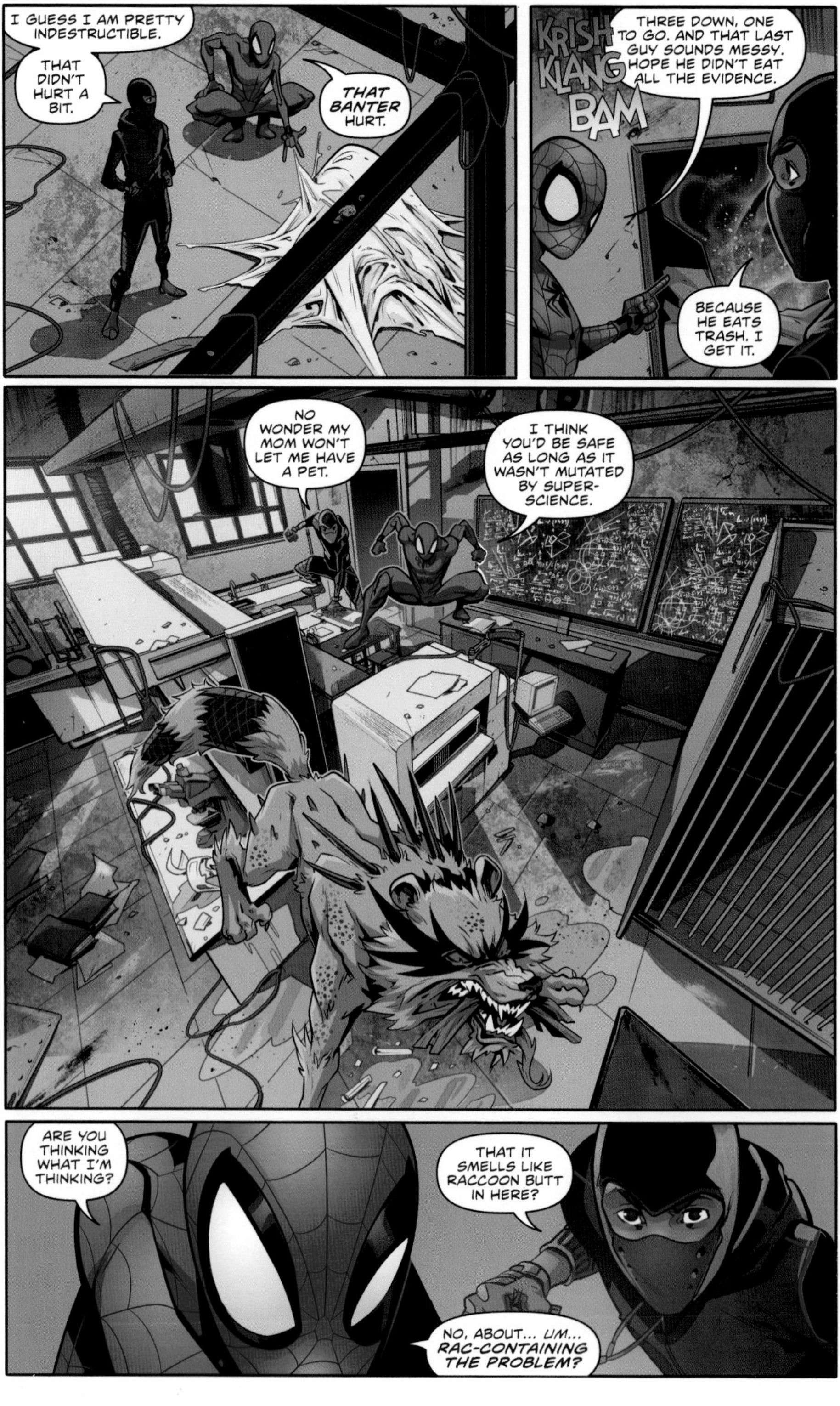

I GUESS I AM PRETTY INDESTRUCTIBLE.
THAT DIDN'T HURT A BIT.
THAT BANTER HURT.
KRISH
KLANG
BAM
THREE DOWN, ONE TO GO. AND THAT LAST GUY SOUNDS MESSY. HOPE HE DIDN'T EAT ALL THE EVIDENCE.
BECAUSE HE EATS TRASH. I GET IT.
NO WONDER MY MOM WON'T LET ME HAVE A PET.
I THINK YOU'D BE SAFE AS LONG AS IT WASN'T MUTATED BY SUPER-SCIENCE.
ARE YOU THINKING WHAT I'M THINKING?
THAT IT SMELLS LIKE RACCOON BUTT IN HERE?
NO, ABOUT... *UM*... *RAC-CONTAINING THE PROBLEM?*

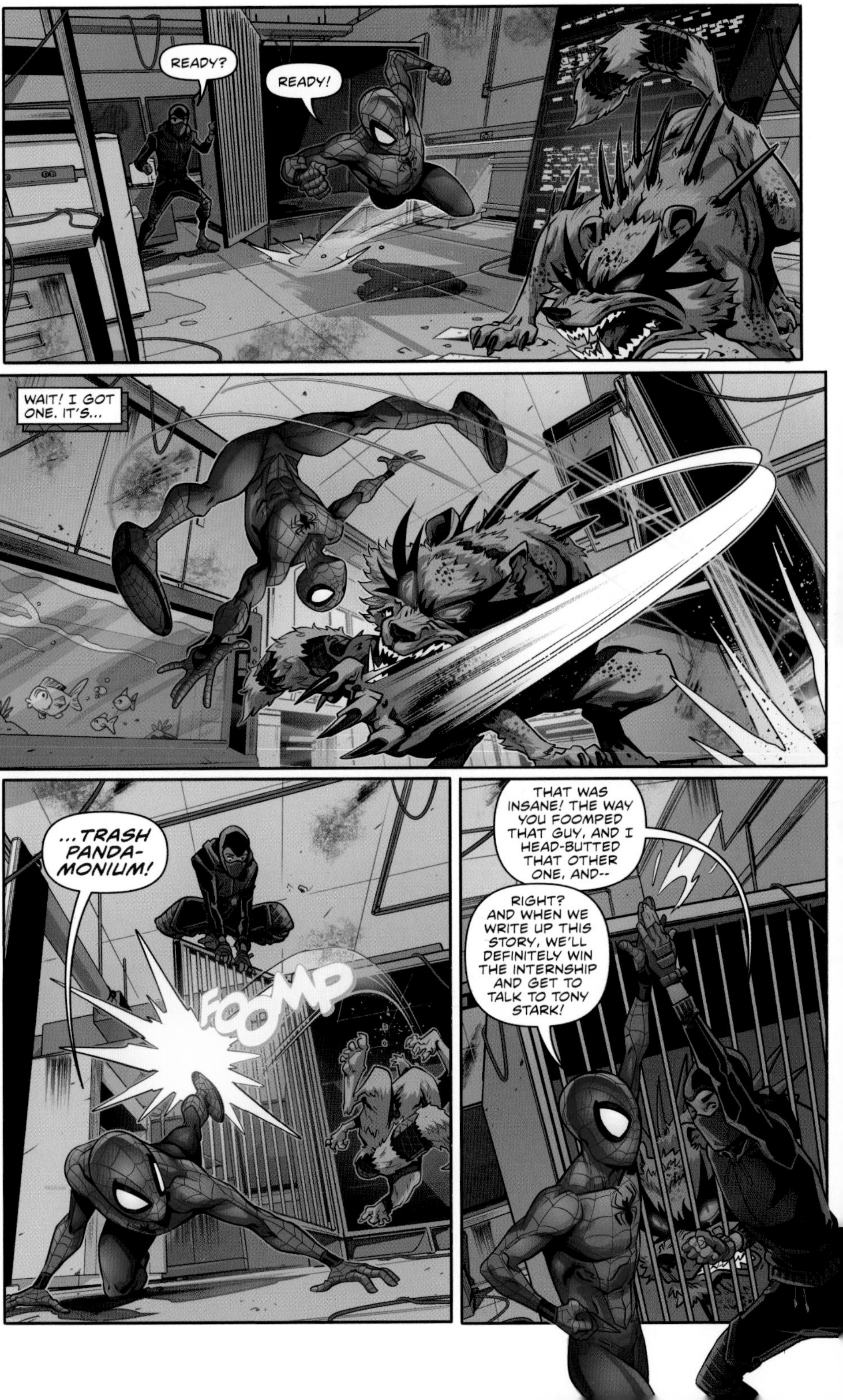
READY?
READY!
WAIT! I GOT ONE. IT'S...
...TRASH PANDA-MONIUM!
FOOMP
THAT WAS INSANE! THE WAY YOU FOOMPED THAT GUY, AND I HEAD-BUTTED THAT OTHER ONE, AND--
RIGHT? AND WHEN WE WRITE UP THIS STORY, WE'LL DEFINITELY WIN THE INTERNSHIP AND GET TO TALK TO TONY STARK!

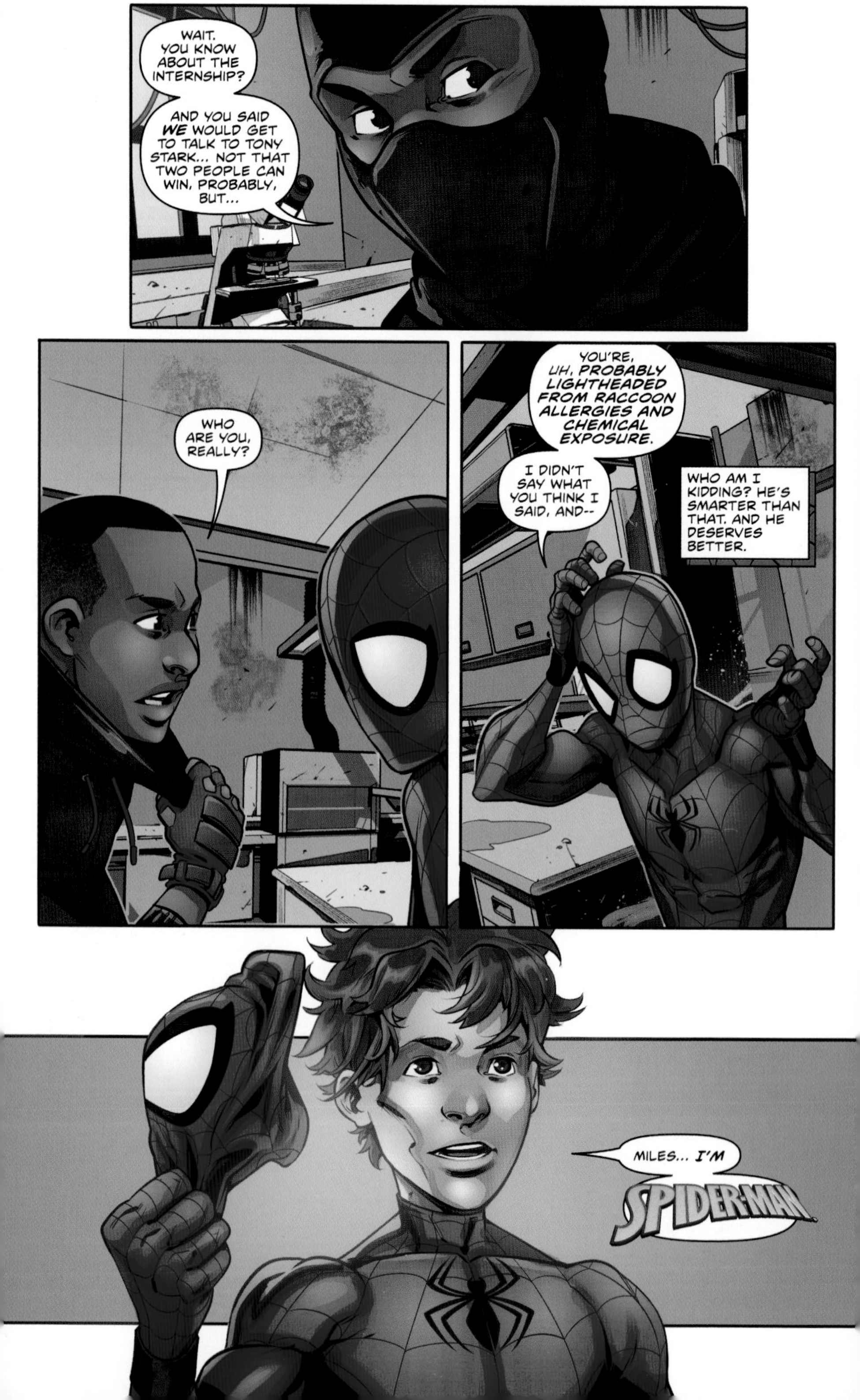
WAIT. YOU KNOW ABOUT THE INTERNSHIP?
AND YOU SAID **WE** WOULD GET TO TALK TO TONY STARK... NOT THAT TWO PEOPLE CAN WIN, PROBABLY, BUT...
WHO ARE YOU, REALLY?
YOU'RE, UH, PROBABLY LIGHTHEADED FROM RACCOON ALLERGIES AND CHEMICAL EXPOSURE.
I DIDN'T SAY WHAT YOU THINK I SAID, AND--
WHO AM I KIDDING? HE'S SMARTER THAN THAT. AND HE DESERVES BETTER.
MILES... I'M
SPIDER-MAN

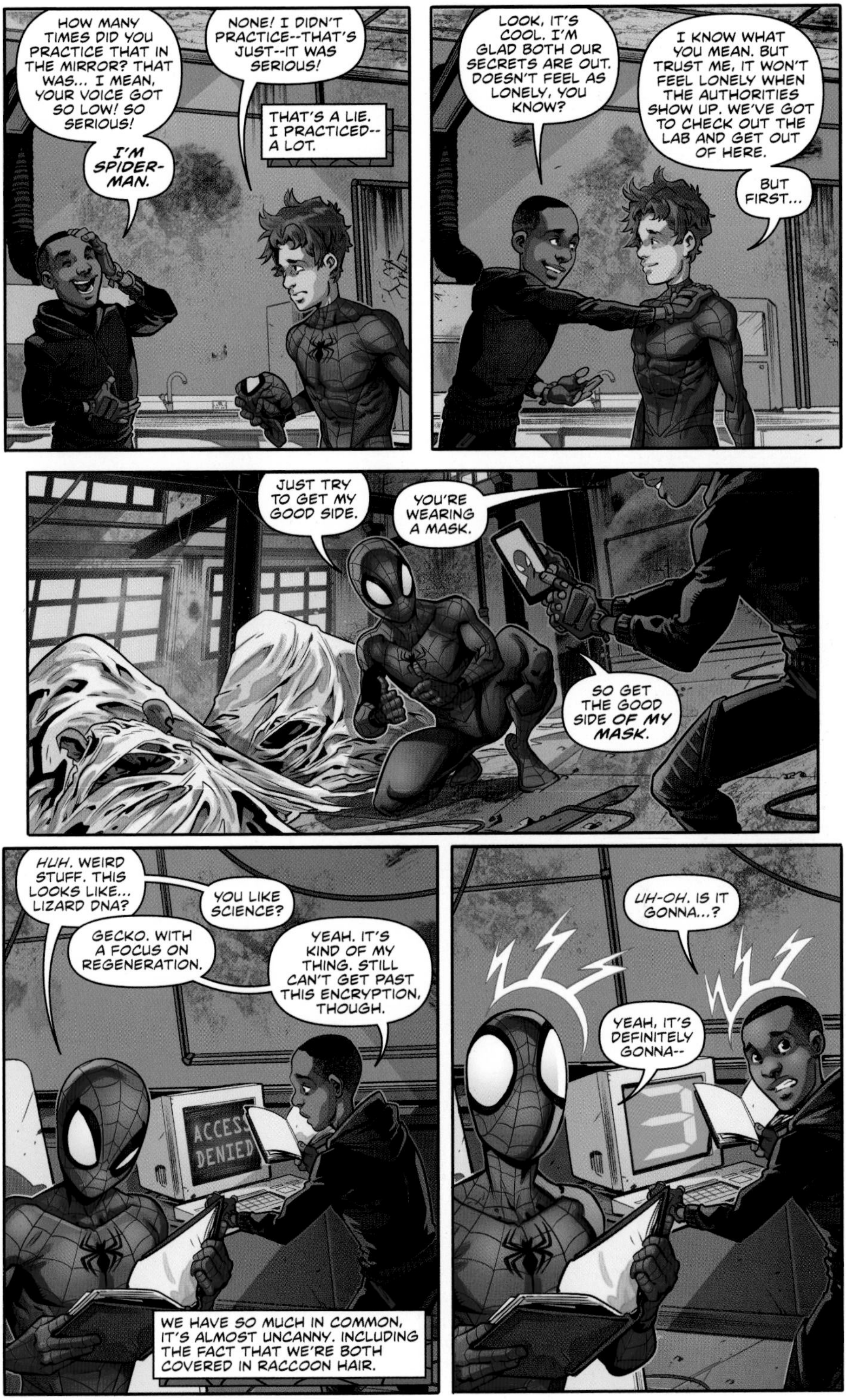
HOW MANY TIMES DID YOU PRACTICE THAT IN THE MIRROR? THAT WAS... I MEAN, YOUR VOICE GOT SO LOW! SO SERIOUS!
I'M SPIDER-MAN.
NONE! I DIDN'T PRACTICE--THAT'S JUST--IT WAS SERIOUS!
THAT'S A LIE. I PRACTICED--A LOT.
LOOK, IT'S COOL. I'M GLAD BOTH OUR SECRETS ARE OUT. DOESN'T FEEL AS LONELY, YOU KNOW?
I KNOW WHAT YOU MEAN. BUT TRUST ME, IT WON'T FEEL LONELY WHEN THE AUTHORITIES SHOW UP. WE'VE GOT TO CHECK OUT THE LAB AND GET OUT OF HERE.
BUT FIRST...
JUST TRY TO GET MY GOOD SIDE.
YOU'RE WEARING A MASK.
SO GET THE GOOD SIDE OF MY MASK.
HUH. WEIRD STUFF. THIS LOOKS LIKE... LIZARD DNA?
YOU LIKE SCIENCE?
GECKO. WITH A FOCUS ON REGENERATION.
YEAH. IT'S KIND OF MY THING. STILL CAN'T GET PAST THIS ENCRYPTION, THOUGH.
ACCESS DENIED
WE HAVE SO MUCH IN COMMON, IT'S ALMOST UNCANNY. INCLUDING THE FACT THAT WE'RE BOTH COVERED IN RACCOON HAIR.
UH-OH. IS IT GONNA...?
YEAH, IT'S DEFINITELY GONNA--
3

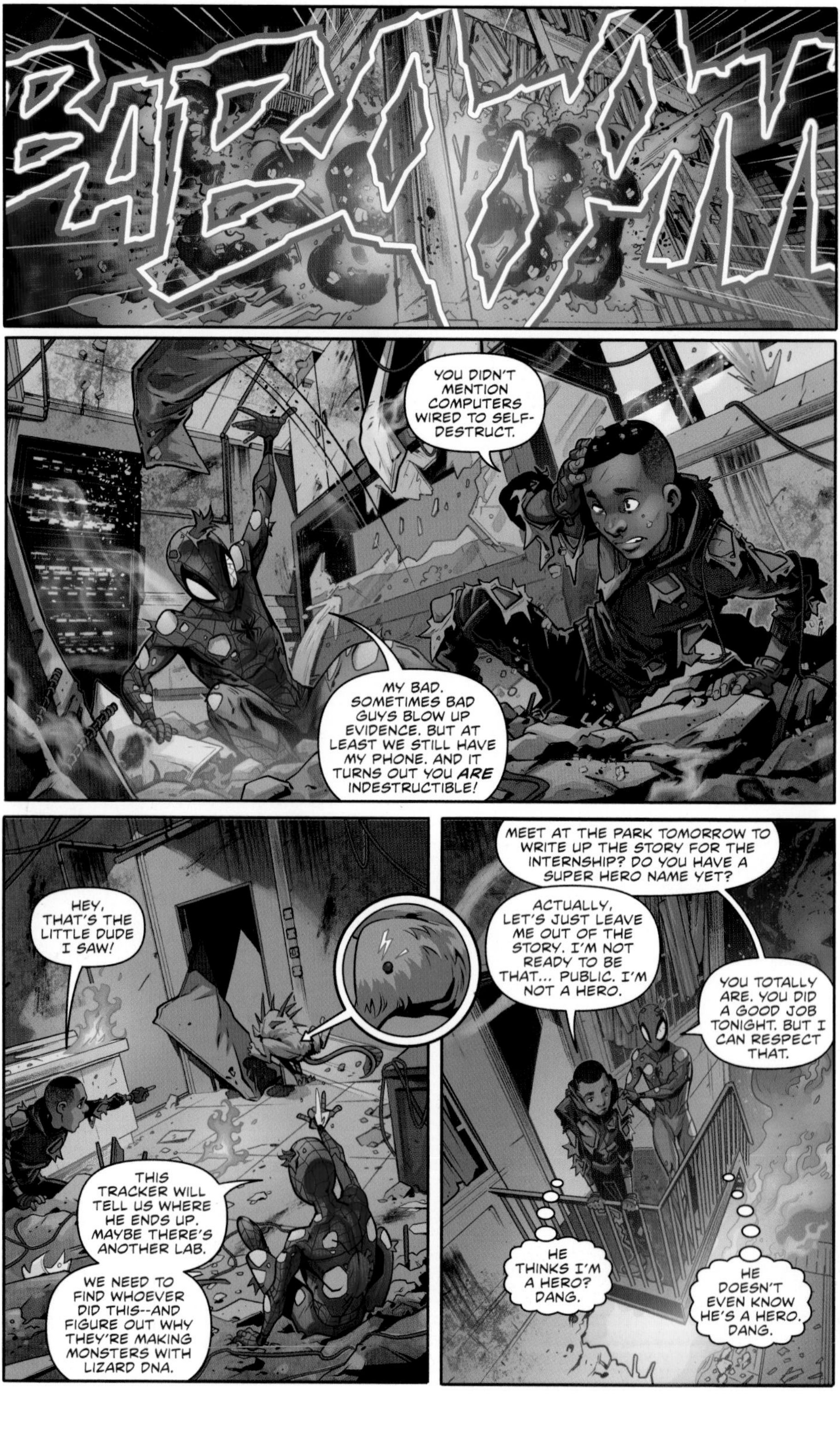
BRZOOM
YOU DIDN'T MENTION COMPUTERS WIRED TO SELF-DESTRUCT.
MY BAD. SOMETIMES BAD GUYS BLOW UP EVIDENCE. BUT AT LEAST WE STILL HAVE MY PHONE. AND IT TURNS OUT YOU *ARE* INDESTRUCTIBLE!
HEY, THAT'S THE LITTLE DUDE I SAW!
THIS TRACKER WILL TELL US WHERE HE ENDS UP. MAYBE THERE'S ANOTHER LAB.
WE NEED TO FIND WHOEVER DID THIS--AND FIGURE OUT WHY THEY'RE MAKING MONSTERS WITH LIZARD DNA.
MEET AT THE PARK TOMORROW TO WRITE UP THE STORY FOR THE INTERNSHIP? DO YOU HAVE A SUPER HERO NAME YET?
ACTUALLY, LET'S JUST LEAVE ME OUT OF THE STORY. I'M NOT READY TO BE THAT... PUBLIC. I'M NOT A HERO.
YOU TOTALLY ARE. YOU DID A GOOD JOB TONIGHT. BUT I CAN RESPECT THAT.
HE THINKS I'M A HERO? DANG.
HE DOESN'T EVEN KNOW HE'S A HERO. DANG.

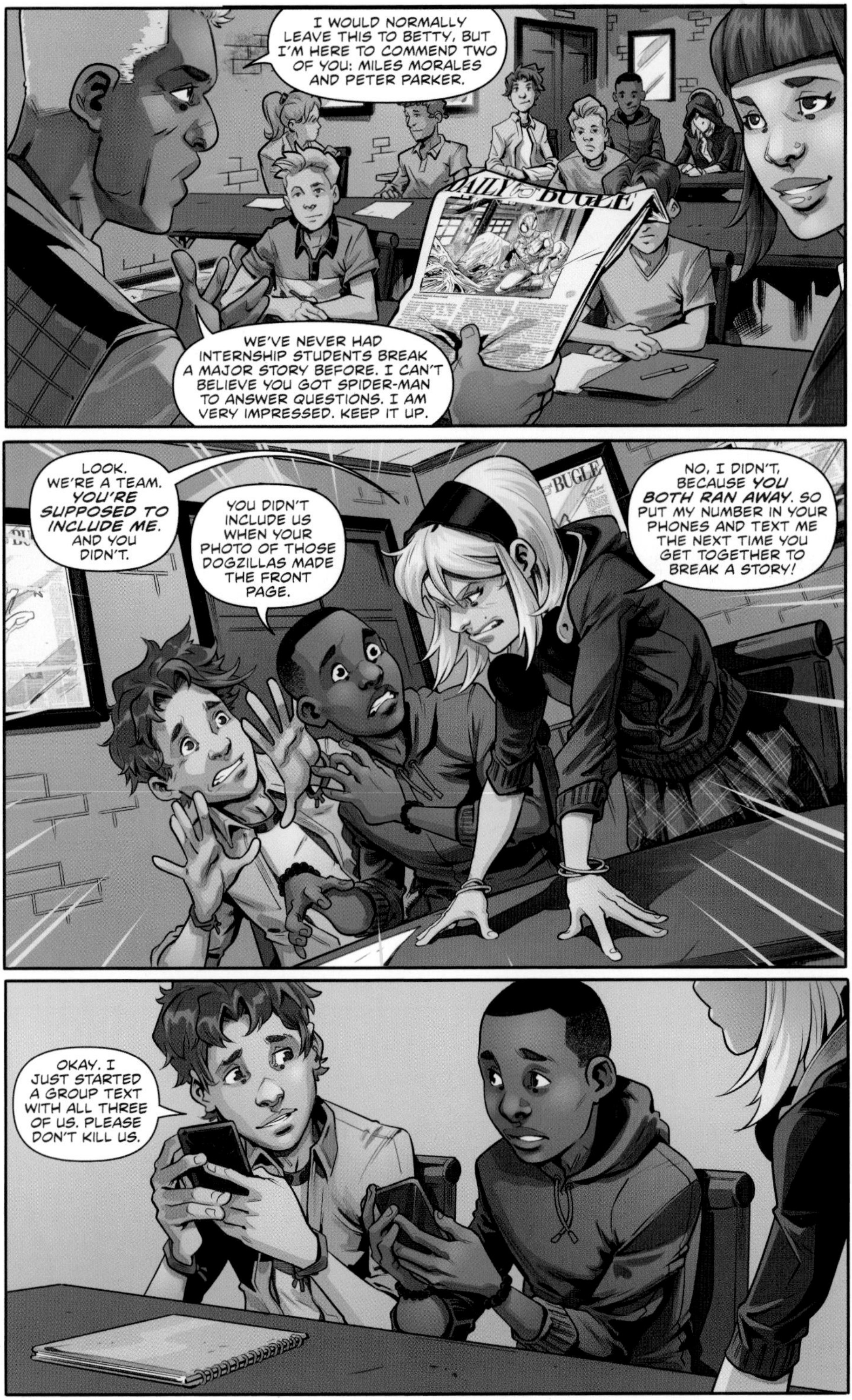
I WOULD NORMALLY LEAVE THIS TO BETTY, BUT I'M HERE TO COMMEND TWO OF YOU: MILES MORALES AND PETER PARKER.
DAILY BUGLE
WE'VE NEVER HAD INTERNSHIP STUDENTS BREAK A MAJOR STORY BEFORE. I CAN'T BELIEVE YOU GOT SPIDER-MAN TO ANSWER QUESTIONS. I AM VERY IMPRESSED. KEEP IT UP.
LOOK. WE'RE A TEAM. *YOU'RE SUPPOSED TO INCLUDE ME*. AND YOU DIDN'T.
YOU DIDN'T INCLUDE US WHEN YOUR PHOTO OF THOSE DOGZILLAS MADE THE FRONT PAGE.
NO, I DIDN'T, BECAUSE *YOU BOTH RAN AWAY*. SO PUT MY NUMBER IN YOUR PHONES AND TEXT ME THE NEXT TIME YOU GET TOGETHER TO BREAK A STORY!
OKAY. I JUST STARTED A GROUP TEXT WITH ALL THREE OF US. PLEASE DON'T KILL US.

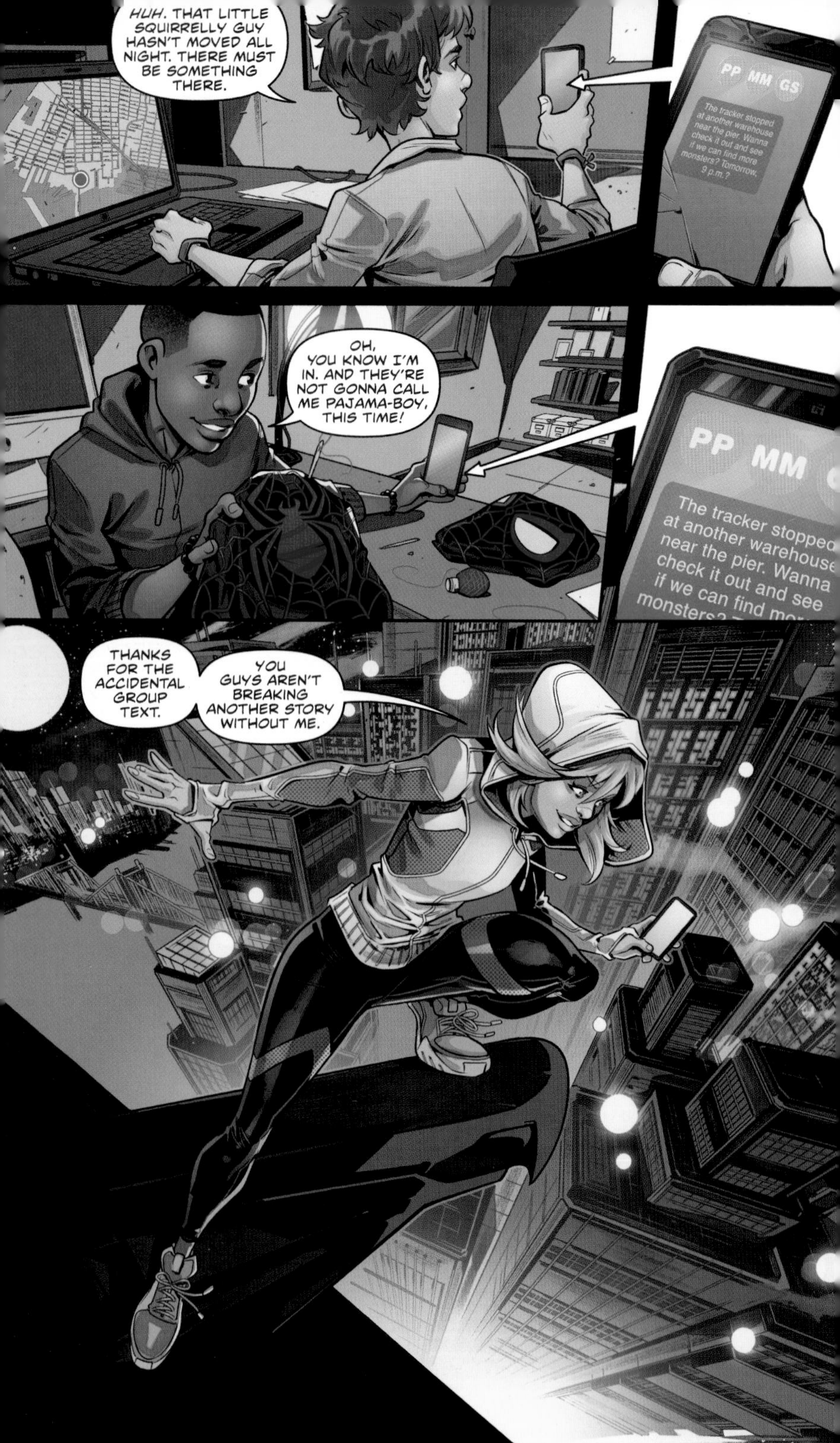

HUH. THAT LITTLE SQUIRRELLY GUY HASN'T MOVED ALL NIGHT. THERE MUST BE SOMETHING THERE.
PP MM GS
The tracker stopped at another warehouse near the pier. Wanna check it out and see if we can find more monsters? Tomorrow, 9 p.m.?
OH, YOU KNOW I'M IN. AND THEY'RE NOT GONNA CALL ME PAJAMA-BOY, THIS TIME!
PP MM
THANKS FOR THE ACCIDENTAL GROUP TEXT.
YOU GUYS AREN'T BREAKING ANOTHER STORY WITHOUT ME.

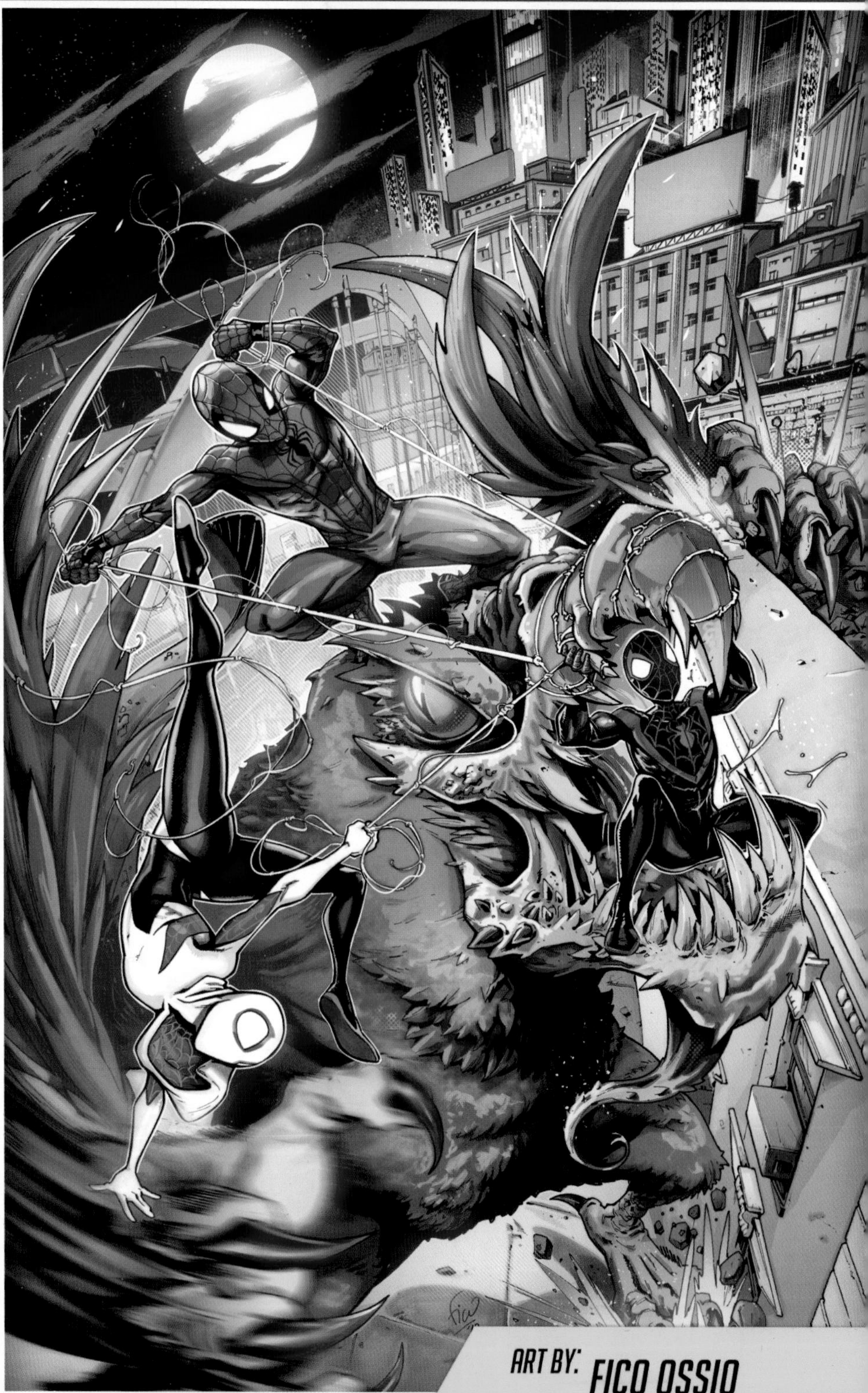

ART BY: FICO OSSIO

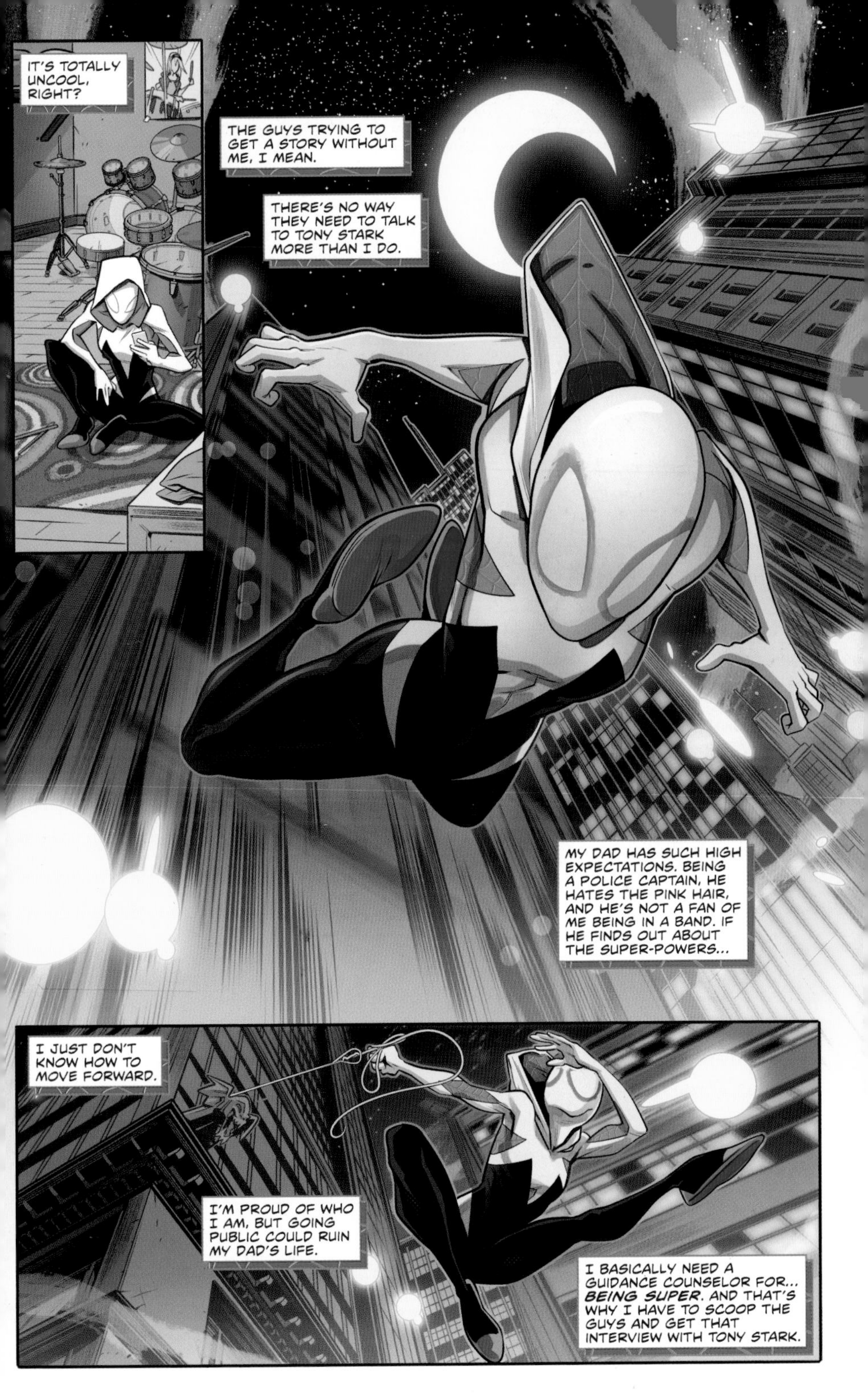
IT'S TOTALLY UNCOOL, RIGHT?
THE GUYS TRYING TO GET A STORY WITHOUT ME, I MEAN.
THERE'S NO WAY THEY NEED TO TALK TO TONY STARK MORE THAN I DO.
MY DAD HAS SUCH HIGH EXPECTATIONS. BEING A POLICE CAPTAIN, HE HATES THE PINK HAIR, AND HE'S NOT A FAN OF ME BEING IN A BAND. IF HE FINDS OUT ABOUT THE SUPER-POWERS...
I JUST DON'T KNOW HOW TO MOVE FORWARD.
I'M PROUD OF WHO I AM, BUT GOING PUBLIC COULD RUIN MY DAD'S LIFE.
I BASICALLY NEED A GUIDANCE COUNSELOR FOR... *BEING SUPER*. AND THAT'S WHY I HAVE TO SCOOP THE GUYS AND GET THAT INTERVIEW WITH TONY STARK.

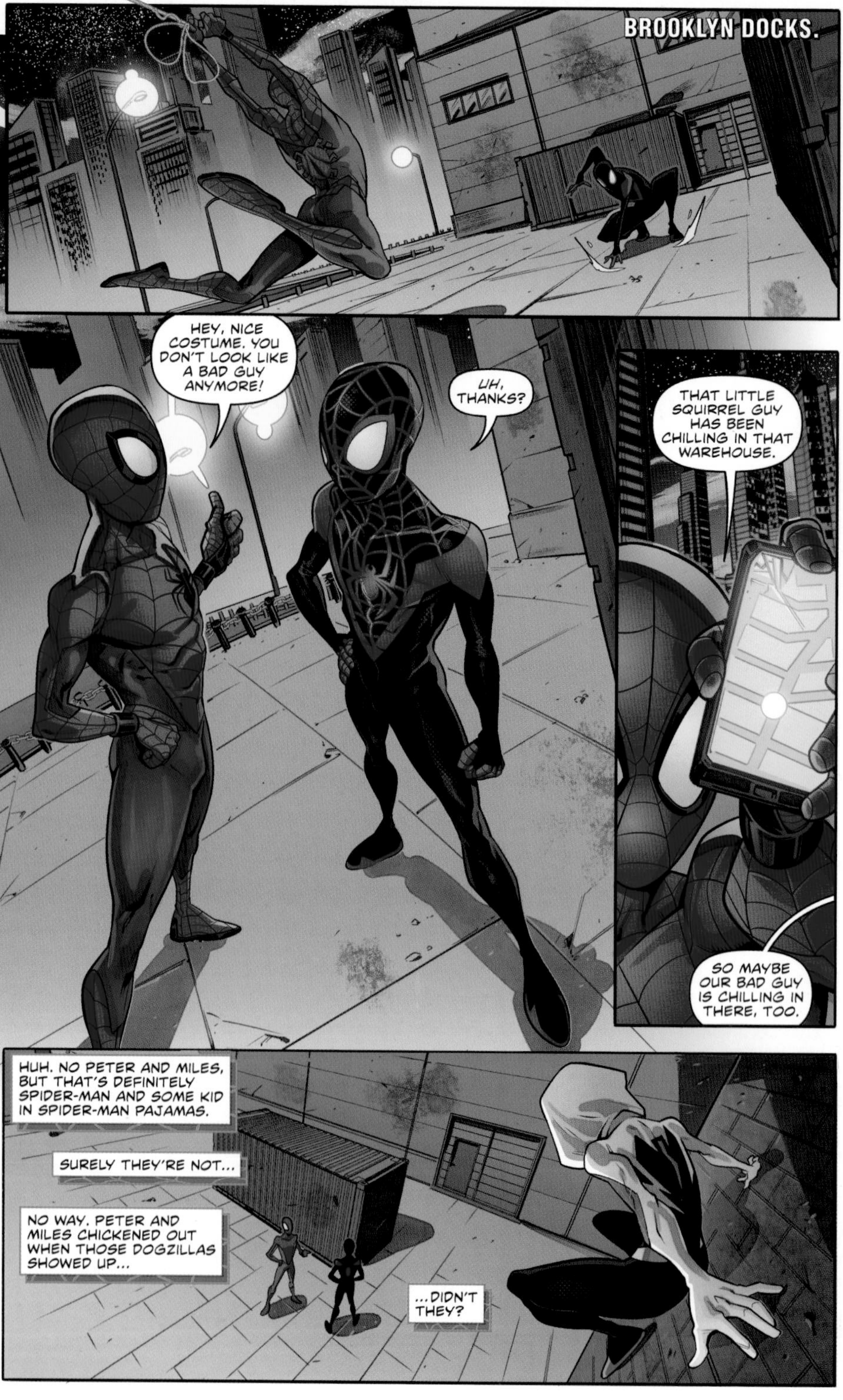

BROOKLYN DOCKS.
HEY, NICE COSTUME. YOU DON'T LOOK LIKE A BAD GUY ANYMORE!
UH, THANKS?
THAT LITTLE SQUIRREL GUY HAS BEEN CHILLING IN THAT WAREHOUSE.
SO MAYBE OUR BAD GUY IS CHILLING IN THERE, TOO.
HUH. NO PETER AND MILES, BUT THAT'S DEFINITELY SPIDER-MAN AND SOME KID IN SPIDER-MAN PAJAMAS.
SURELY THEY'RE NOT...
NO WAY. PETER AND MILES CHICKENED OUT WHEN THOSE DOGZILLAS SHOWED UP...
...DIDN'T THEY?

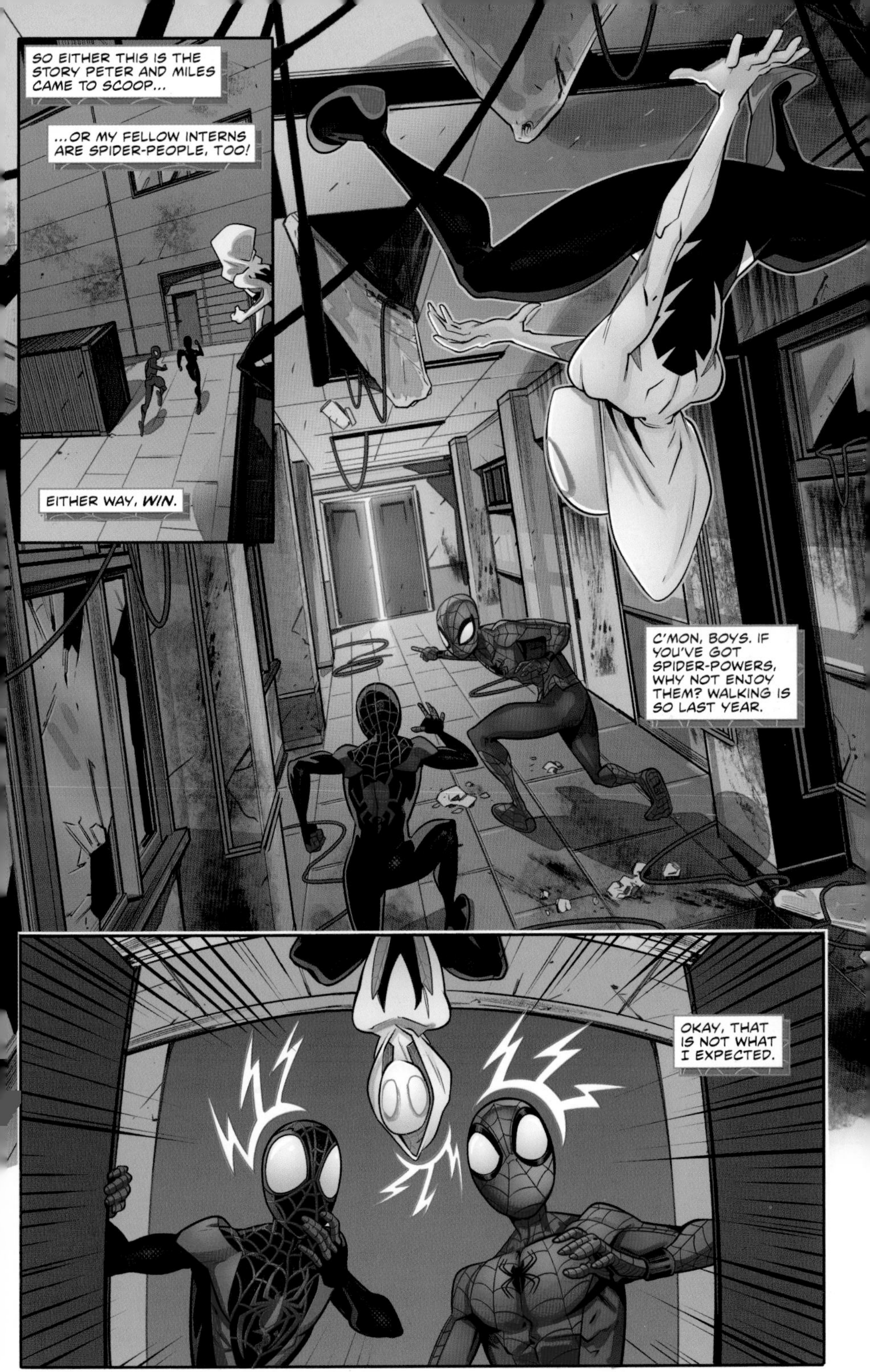
SO EITHER THIS IS THE STORY PETER AND MILES CAME TO SCOOP...
...OR MY FELLOW INTERNS ARE SPIDER-PEOPLE, TOO!
EITHER WAY, *WIN*.
C'MON, BOYS. IF YOU'VE GOT SPIDER-POWERS, WHY NOT ENJOY THEM? WALKING IS SO LAST YEAR.
OKAY, THAT IS NOT WHAT I EXPECTED.

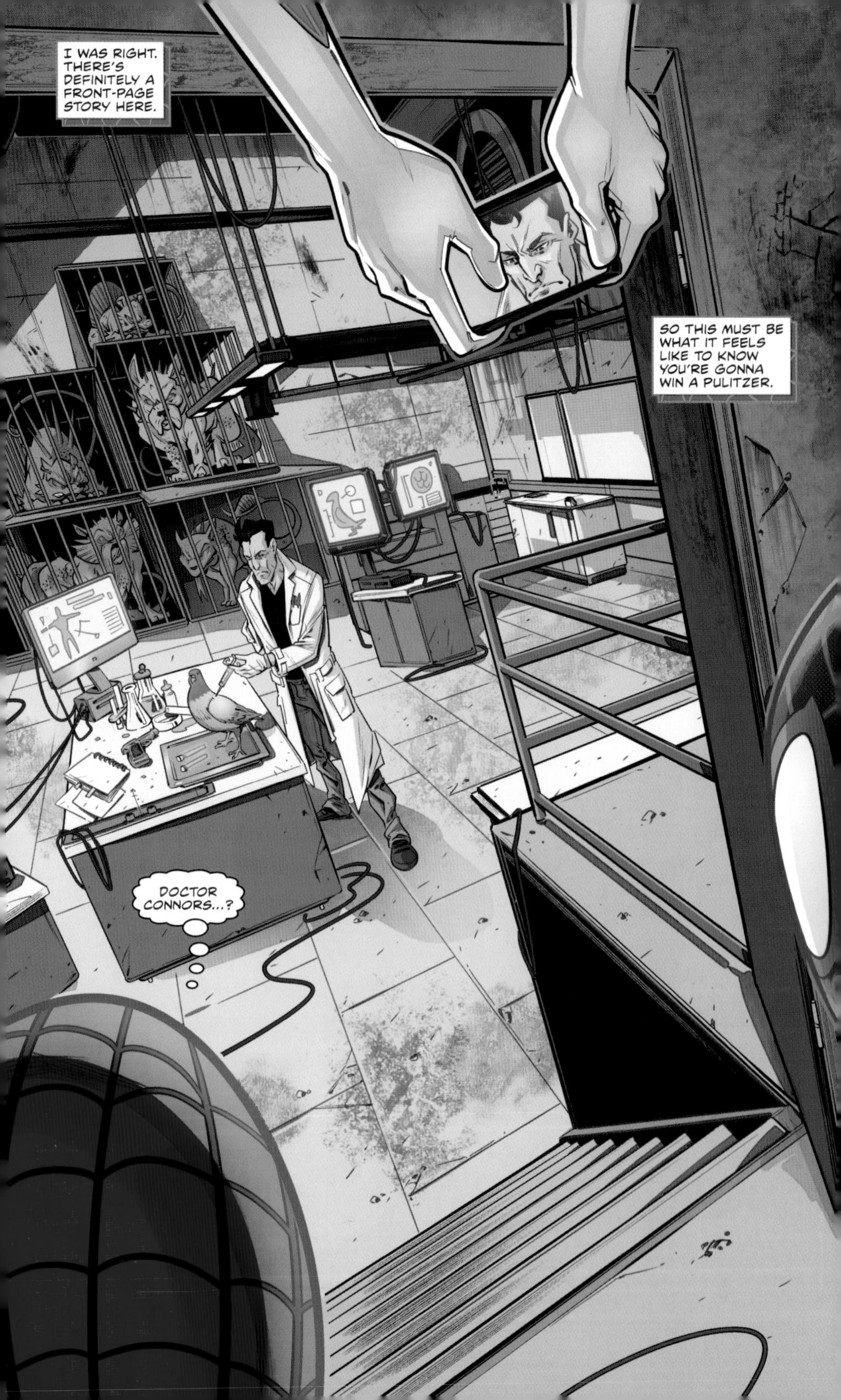
I WAS RIGHT. THERE'S DEFINITELY A FRONT-PAGE STORY HERE.
SO THIS MUST BE WHAT IT FEELS LIKE TO KNOW YOU'RE GONNA WIN A PULITZER.
DOCTOR CONNORS...?

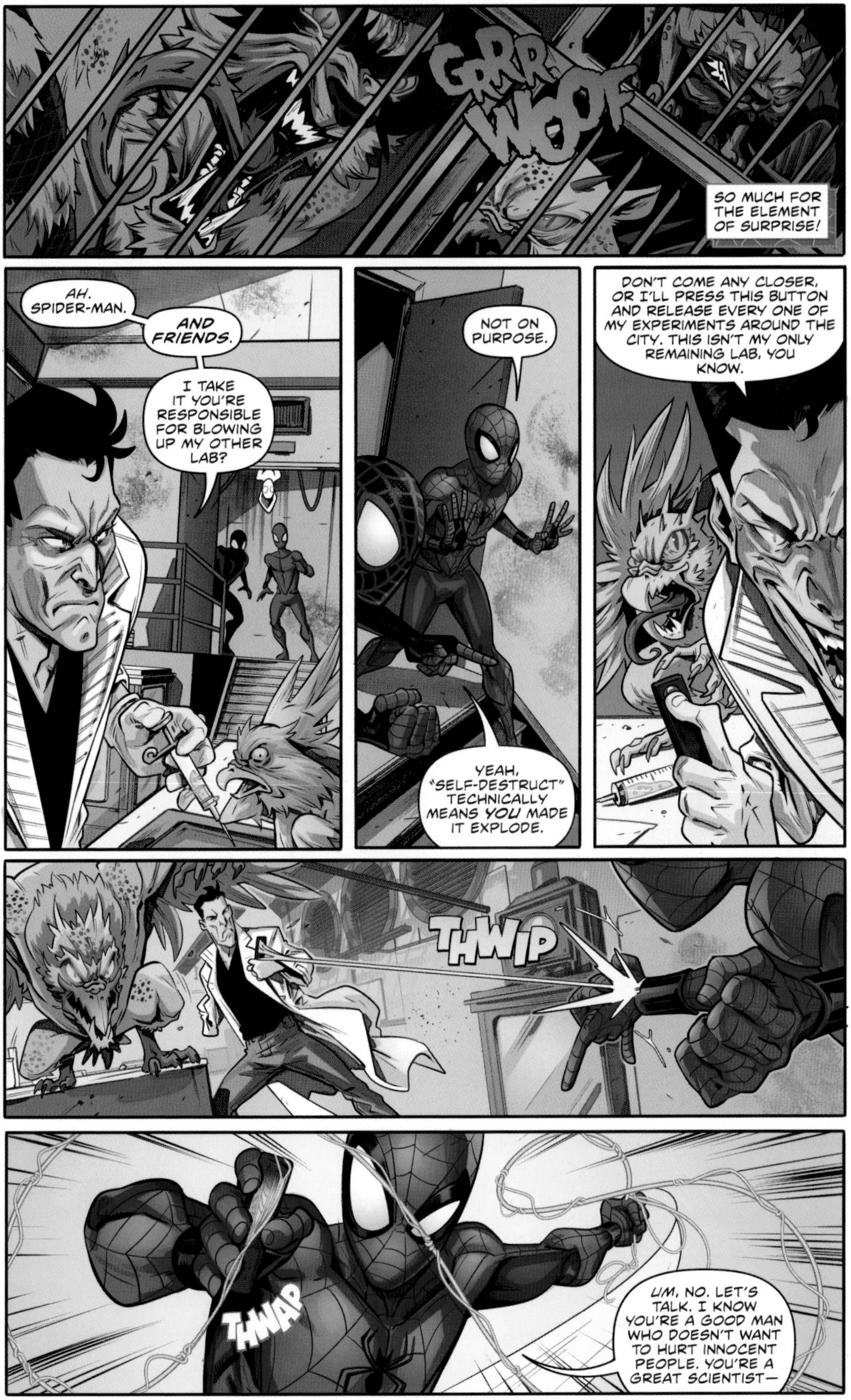
GRR WOOF
SO MUCH FOR THE ELEMENT OF SURPRISE!
AH. SPIDER-MAN.
AND FRIENDS.
I TAKE IT YOU'RE RESPONSIBLE FOR BLOWING UP MY OTHER LAB?
NOT ON PURPOSE.
YEAH, "SELF-DESTRUCT" TECHNICALLY MEANS YOU MADE IT EXPLODE.
DON'T COME ANY CLOSER, OR I'LL PRESS THIS BUTTON AND RELEASE EVERY ONE OF MY EXPERIMENTS AROUND THE CITY. THIS ISN'T MY ONLY REMAINING LAB, YOU KNOW.
THWIP
THWAP
UM, NO. LET'S TALK. I KNOW YOU'RE A GOOD MAN WHO DOESN'T WANT TO HURT INNOCENT PEOPLE. YOU'RE A GREAT SCIENTIST—

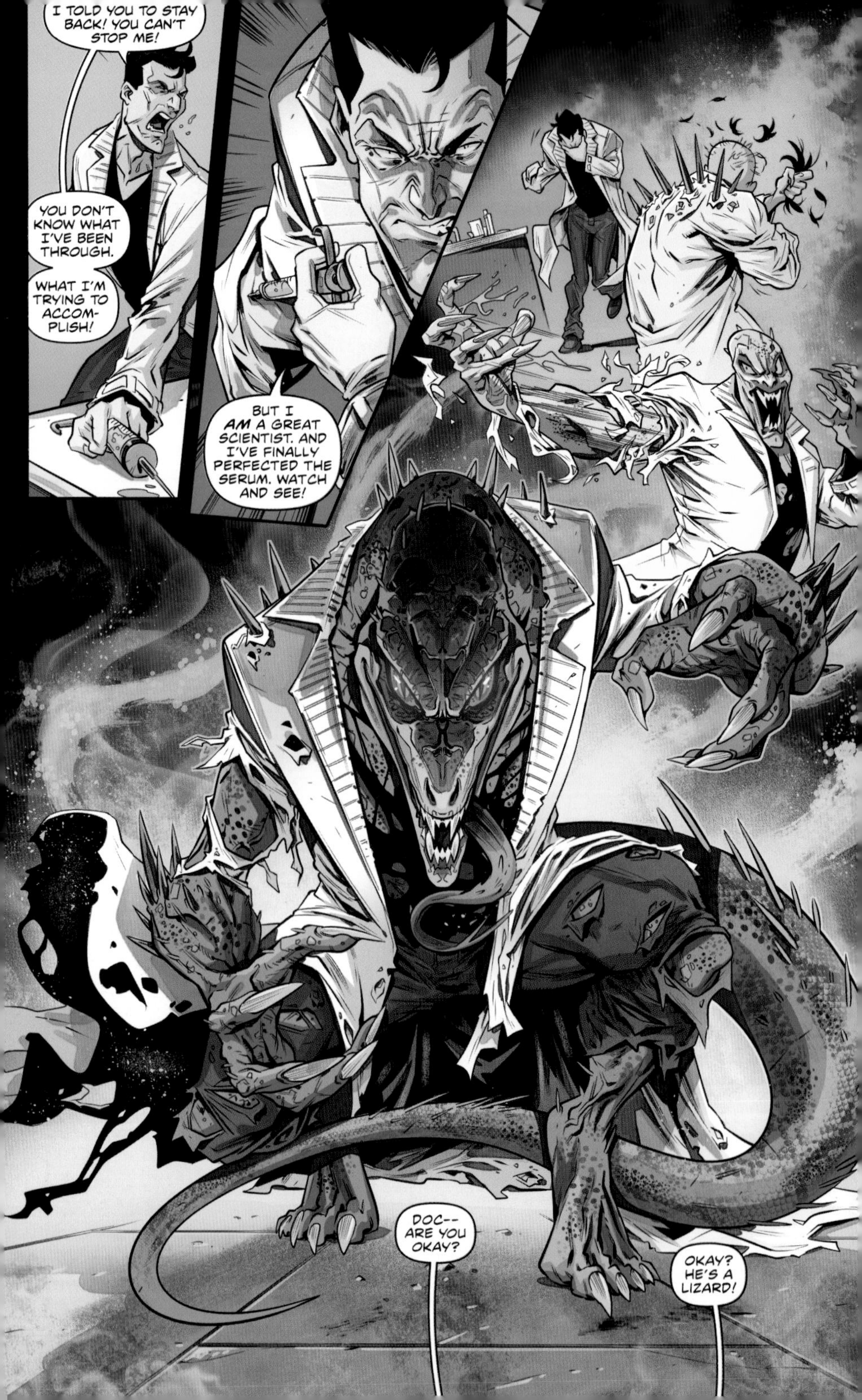
I TOLD YOU TO STAY BACK! YOU CAN'T STOP ME!
YOU DON'T KNOW WHAT I'VE BEEN THROUGH.
WHAT I'M TRYING TO ACCOMPLISH!
BUT I **AM** A GREAT SCIENTIST. AND I'VE FINALLY PERFECTED THE SERUM. WATCH AND SEE!
DOC-- ARE YOU OKAY?
OKAY? HE'S A LIZARD!

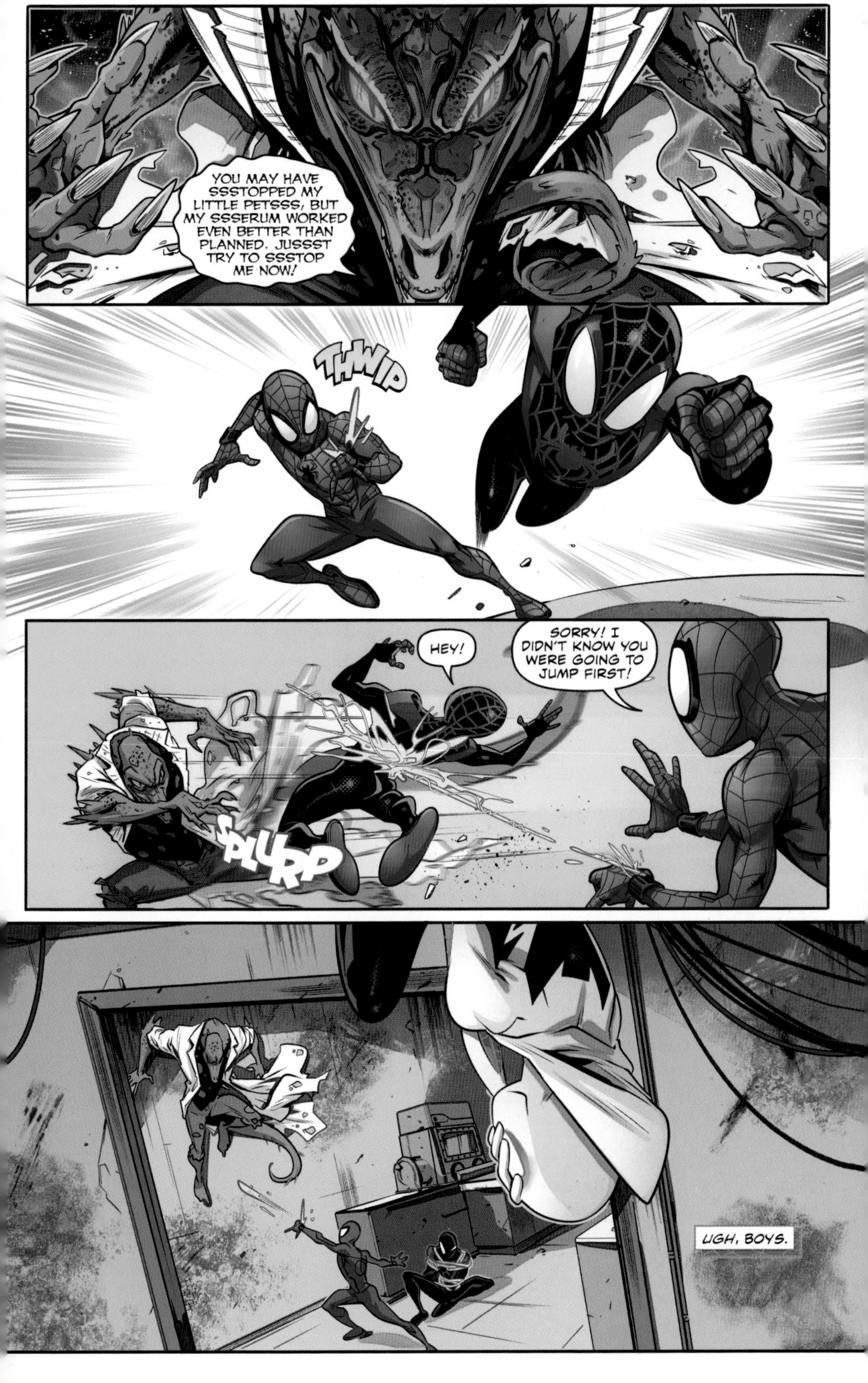
YOU MAY HAVE SSSTOPPED MY LITTLE PETSSS, BUT MY SSSERUM WORKED EVEN BETTER THAN PLANNED. JUSSST TRY TO SSSTOP ME NOW!
THWIP
HEY!
SORRY! I DIDN'T KNOW YOU WERE GOING TO JUMP FIRST!
SPLURP
UGH, BOYS.

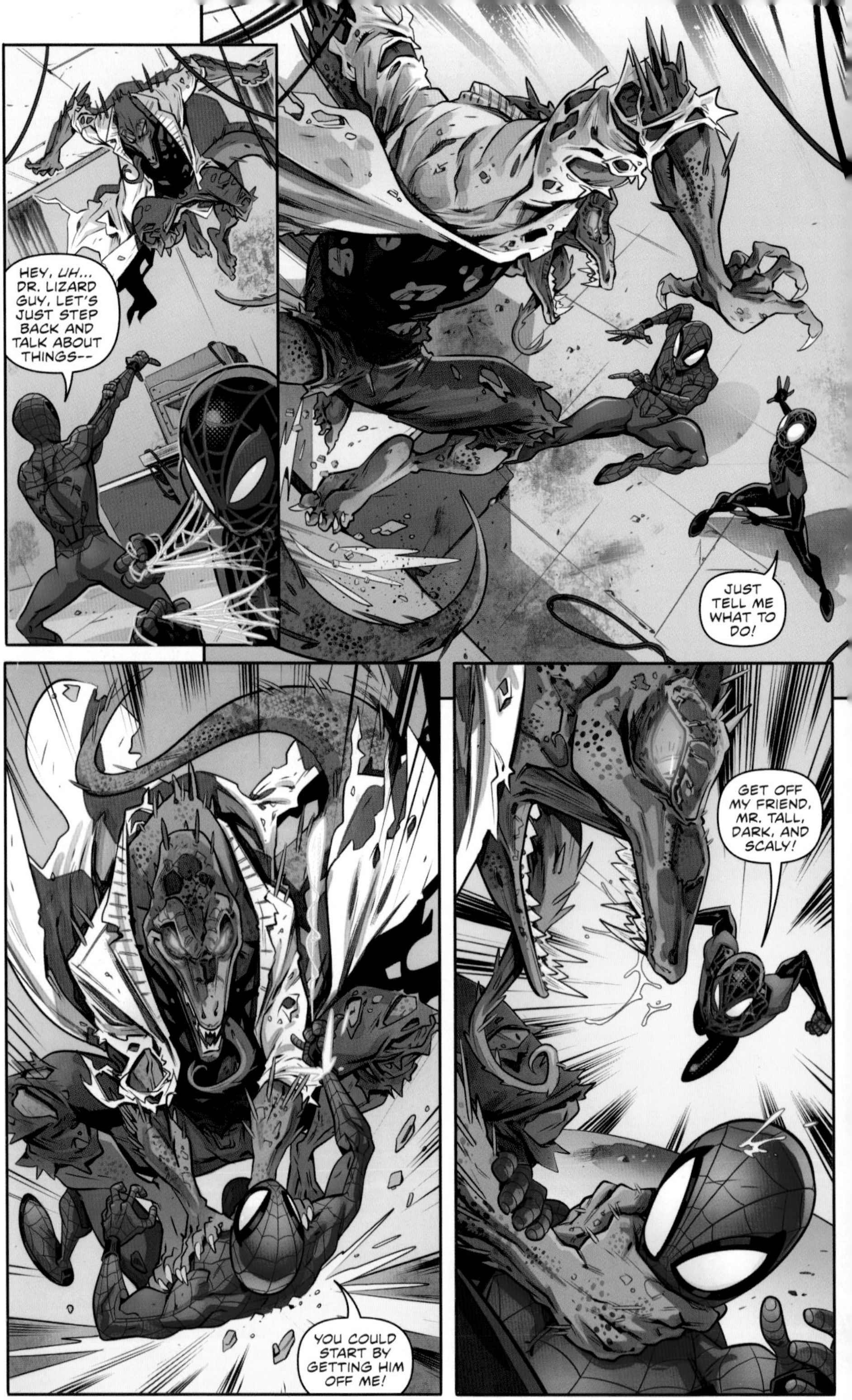
HEY, UH... DR. LIZARD GUY, LET'S JUST STEP BACK AND TALK ABOUT THINGS--
JUST TELL ME WHAT TO DO!
YOU COULD START BY GETTING HIM OFF ME!
GET OFF MY FRIEND, MR. TALL, DARK, AND SCALY!

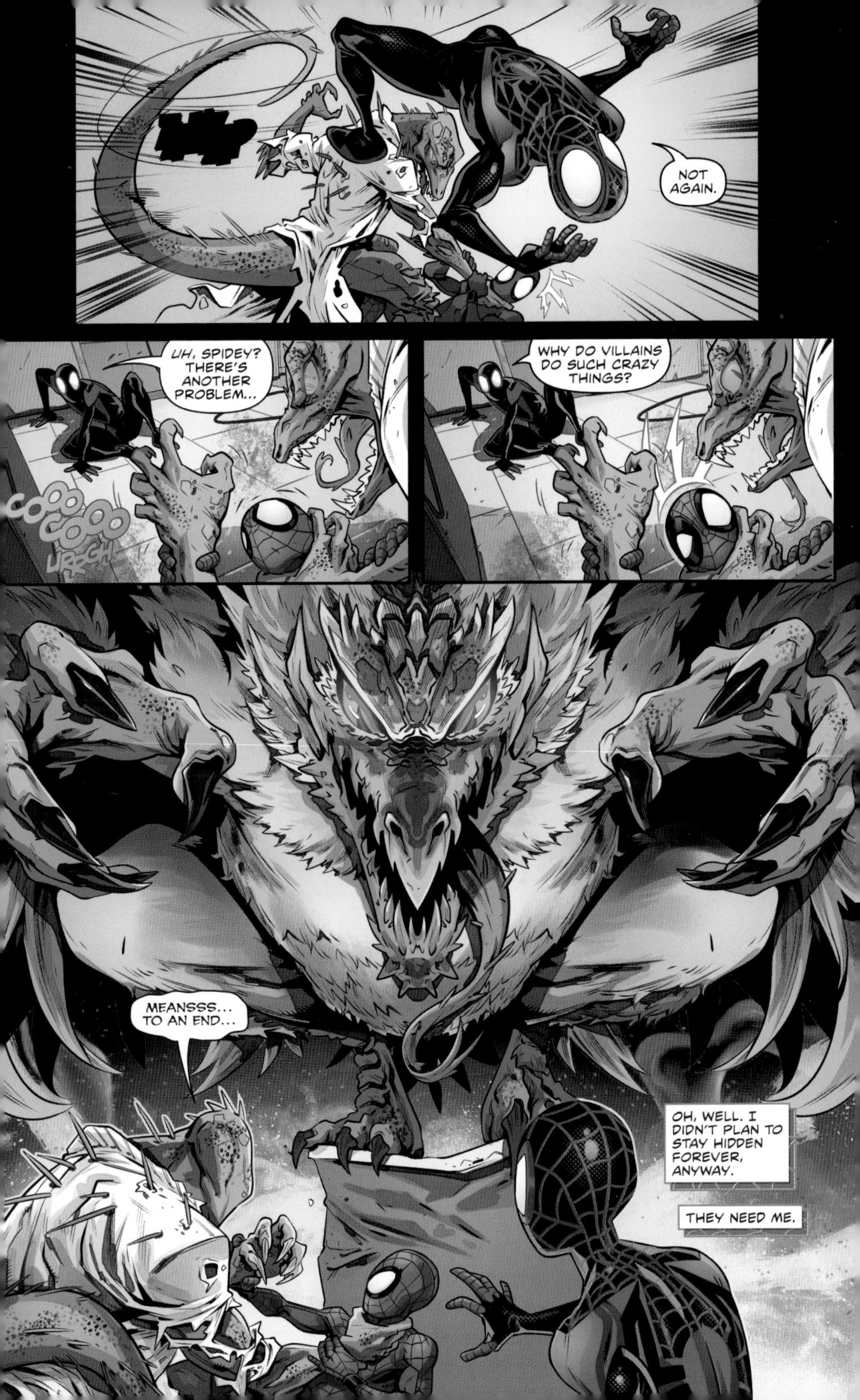
[redacted]
NOT AGAIN.
UH, SPIDEY? THERE'S ANOTHER PROBLEM...
URRGH
WHY DO VILLAINS DO SUCH CRAZY THINGS?
MEANSSS... TO AN END...
OH, WELL. I DIDN'T PLAN TO STAY HIDDEN FOREVER, ANYWAY.
THEY NEED ME.

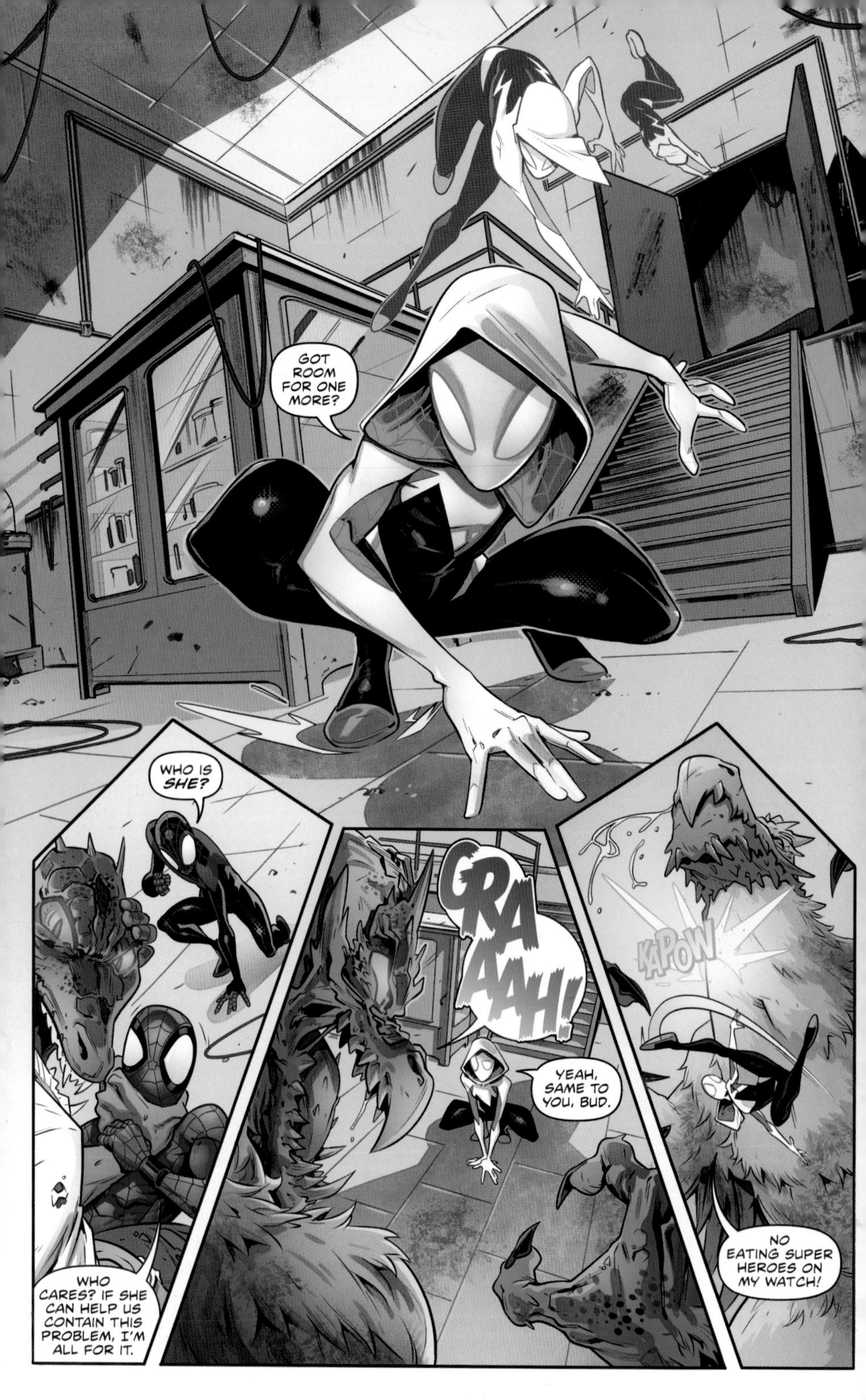
GOT ROOM FOR ONE MORE?
WHO IS SHE?
WHO CARES? IF SHE CAN HELP US CONTAIN THIS PROBLEM, I'M ALL FOR IT.
GRAAAH!
YEAH, SAME TO YOU, BUD.
KAPOW
NO EATING SUPER HEROES ON MY WATCH!

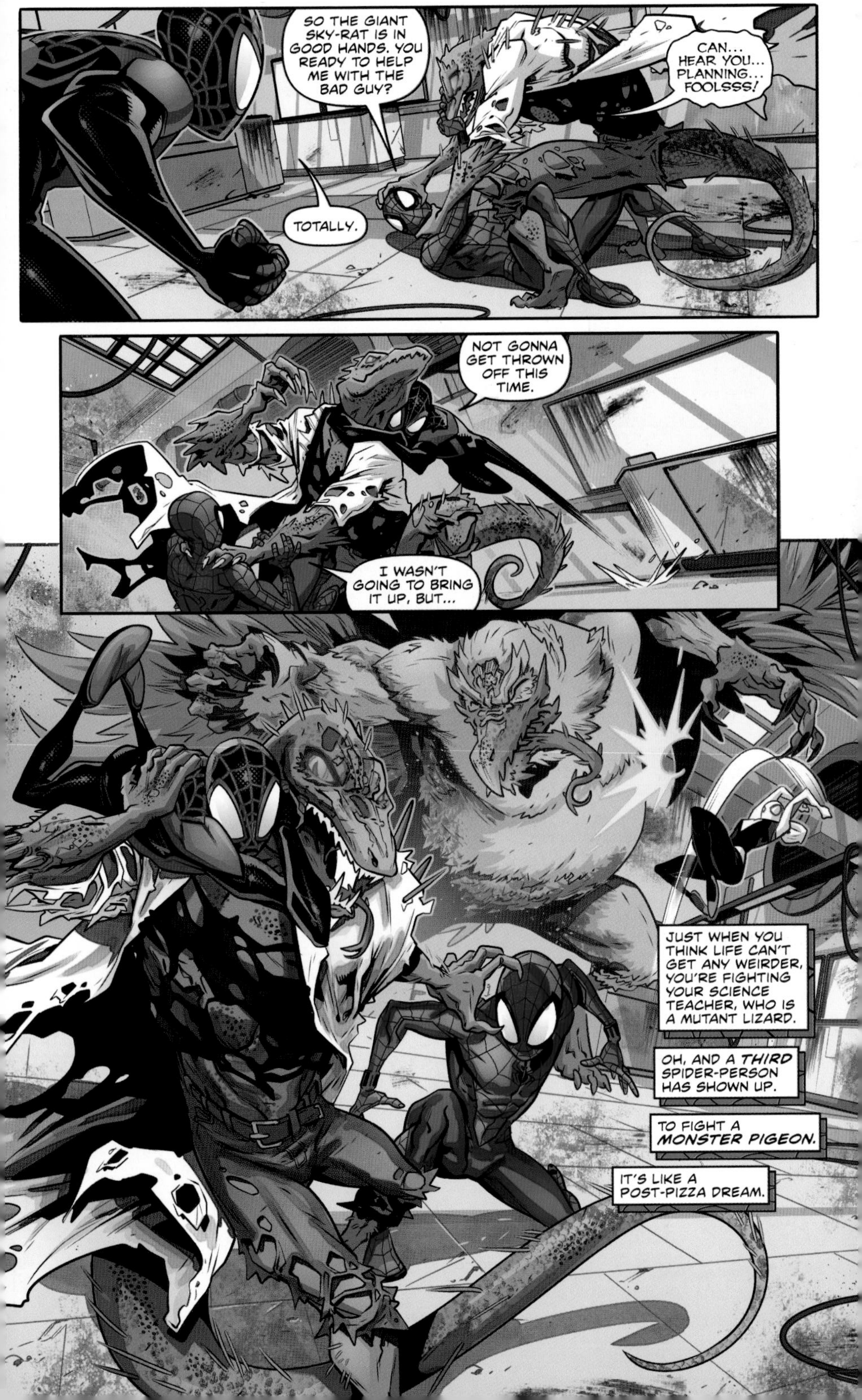
SO THE GIANT SKY-RAT IS IN GOOD HANDS. YOU READY TO HELP ME WITH THE BAD GUY?
TOTALLY.
CAN... HEAR YOU... PLANNING... FOOLSSS!
NOT GONNA GET THROWN OFF THIS TIME.
I WASN'T GOING TO BRING IT UP, BUT...
JUST WHEN YOU THINK LIFE CAN'T GET ANY WEIRDER, YOU'RE FIGHTING YOUR SCIENCE TEACHER, WHO IS A MUTANT LIZARD.
OH, AND A *THIRD* SPIDER-PERSON HAS SHOWN UP.
TO FIGHT A ***MONSTER PIGEON***.
IT'S LIKE A POST-PIZZA DREAM.

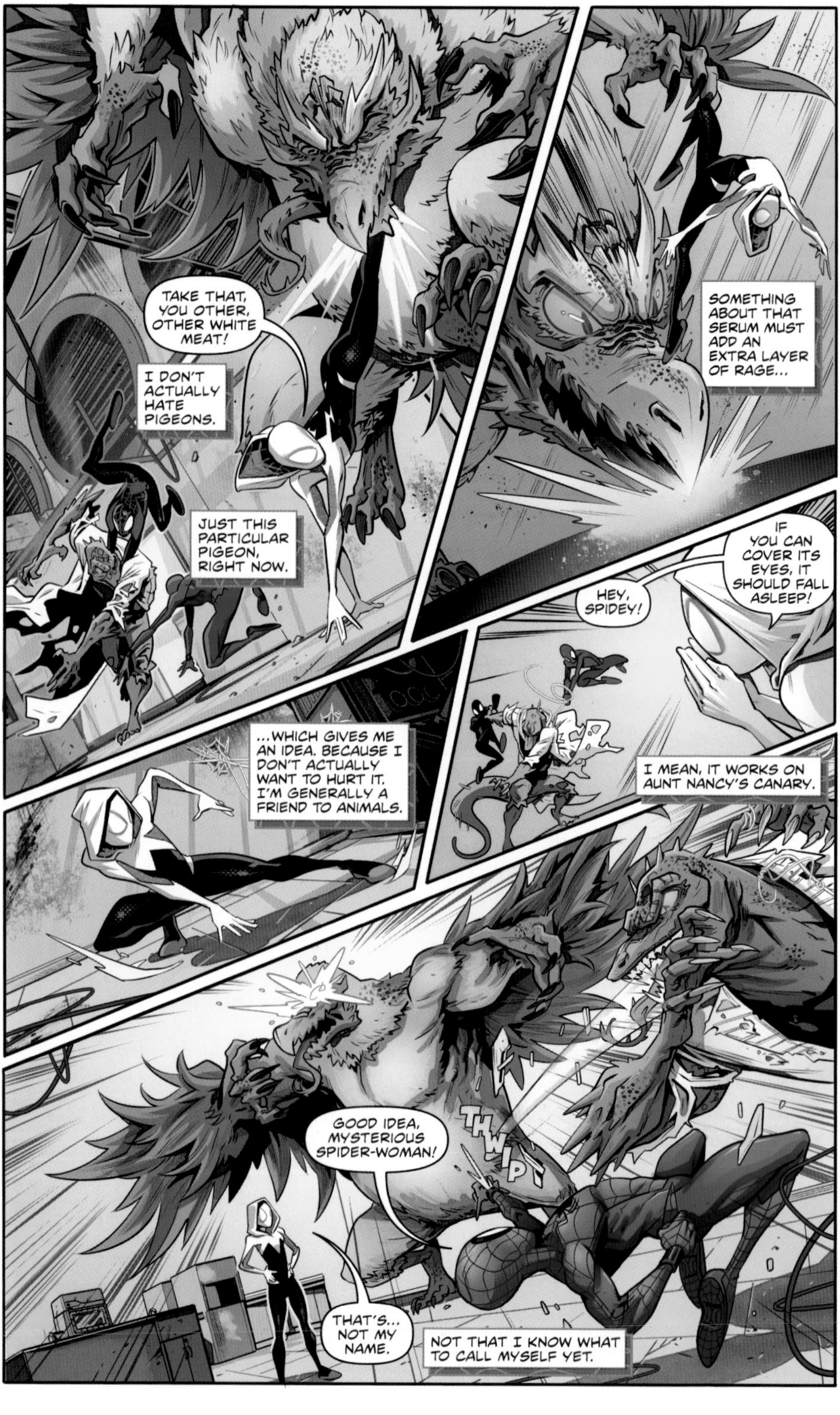
TAKE THAT, YOU OTHER, OTHER WHITE MEAT!
I DON'T ACTUALLY HATE PIGEONS.
JUST THIS PARTICULAR PIGEON, RIGHT NOW.
SOMETHING ABOUT THAT SERUM MUST ADD AN EXTRA LAYER OF RAGE...
...WHICH GIVES ME AN IDEA. BECAUSE I DON'T ACTUALLY WANT TO HURT IT. I'M GENERALLY A FRIEND TO ANIMALS.
HEY, SPIDEY!
IF YOU CAN COVER ITS EYES, IT SHOULD FALL ASLEEP!
I MEAN, IT WORKS ON AUNT NANCY'S CANARY.
GOOD IDEA, MYSTERIOUS SPIDER-WOMAN!
THWIP
THAT'S... NOT MY NAME.
NOT THAT I KNOW WHAT TO CALL MYSELF YET.

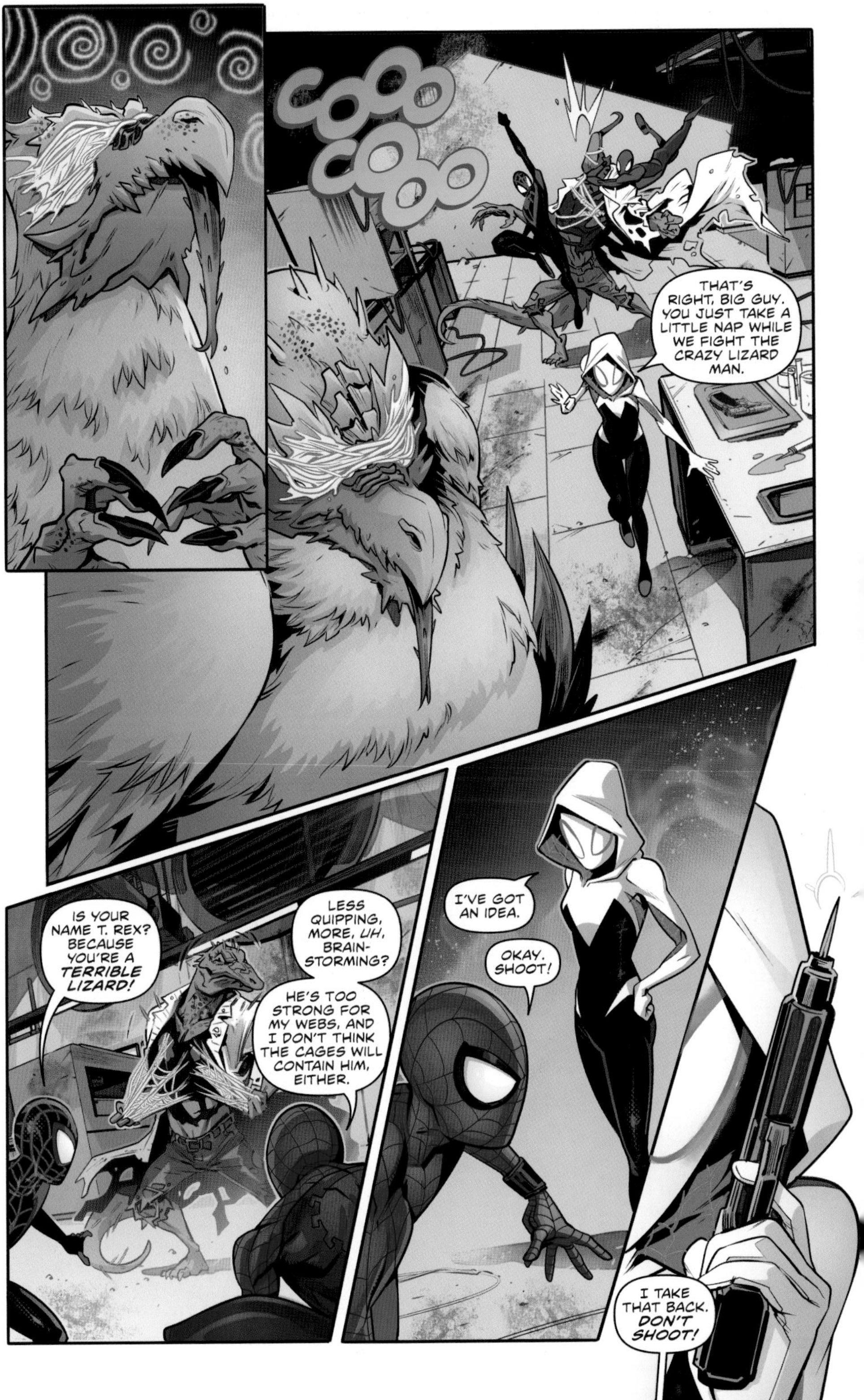
COO COO
COO COO
THAT'S RIGHT, BIG GUY. YOU JUST TAKE A LITTLE NAP WHILE WE FIGHT THE CRAZY LIZARD MAN.
IS YOUR NAME T. REX? BECAUSE YOU'RE A *TERRIBLE LIZARD!*
LESS QUIPPING, MORE, *UH*, BRAIN-STORMING?
HE'S TOO STRONG FOR MY WEBS, AND I DON'T THINK THE CAGES WILL CONTAIN HIM, EITHER.
I'VE GOT AN IDEA.
OKAY. SHOOT!
I TAKE THAT BACK. ***DON'T SHOOT!***

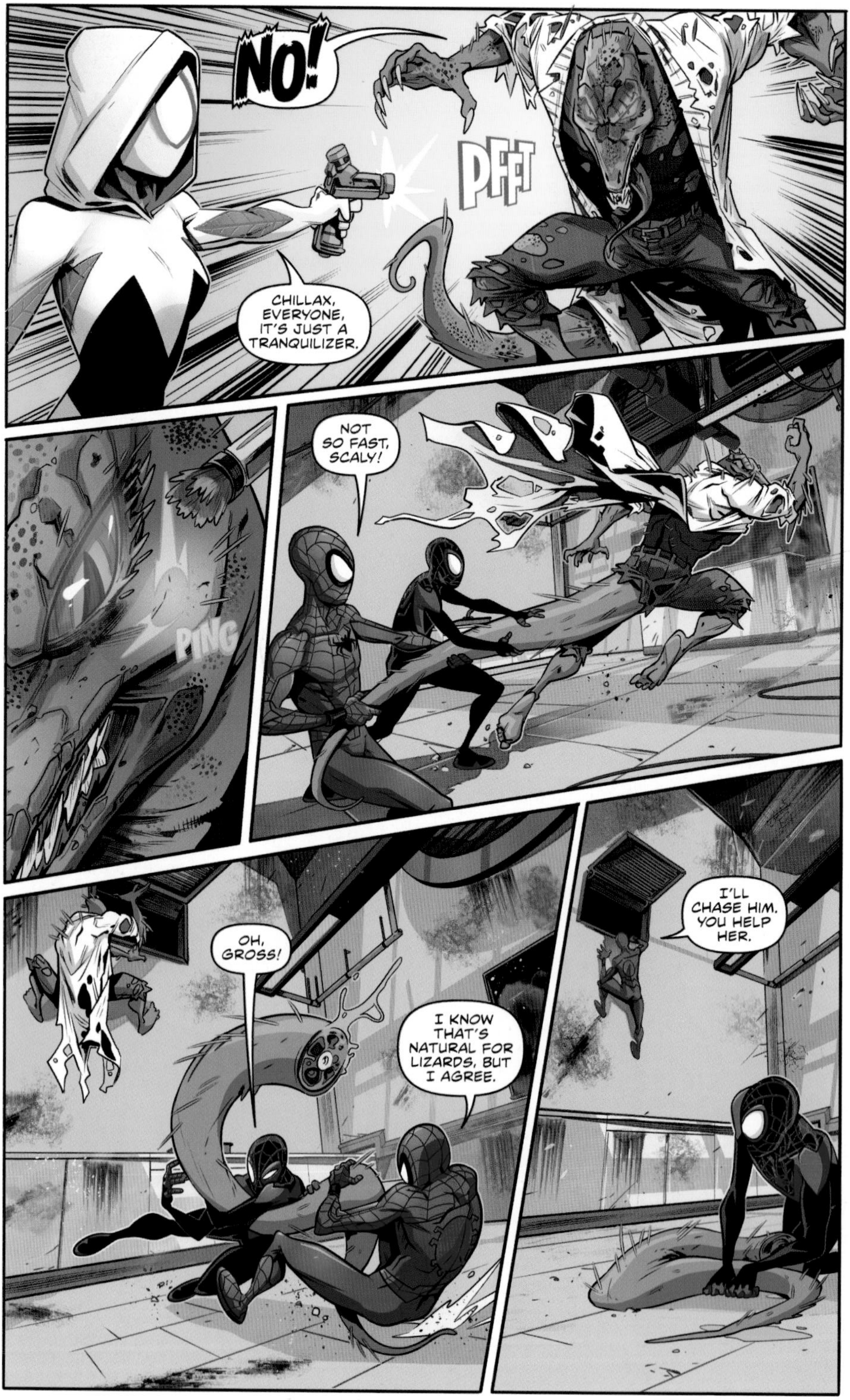
NO!
PFFT
CHILLAX, EVERYONE, IT'S JUST A TRANQUILIZER.
PING
NOT SO FAST, SCALY!
OH, GROSS!
I KNOW THAT'S NATURAL FOR LIZARDS, BUT I AGREE.
I'LL CHASE HIM. YOU HELP HER.

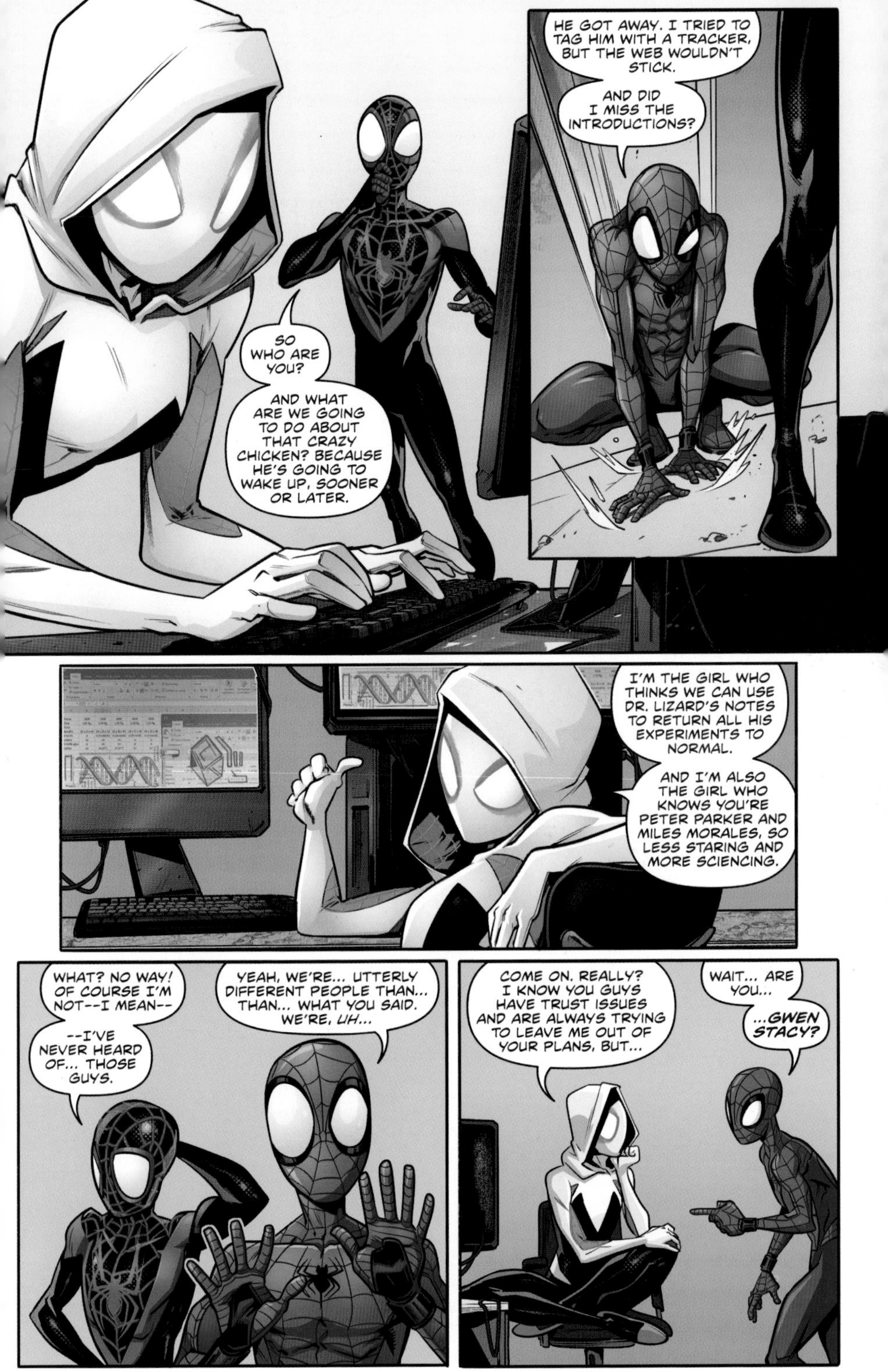
HE GOT AWAY. I TRIED TO TAG HIM WITH A TRACKER, BUT THE WEB WOULDN'T STICK.
AND DID I MISS THE INTRODUCTIONS?
SO WHO ARE YOU?
AND WHAT ARE WE GOING TO DO ABOUT THAT CRAZY CHICKEN? BECAUSE HE'S GOING TO WAKE UP, SOONER OR LATER.
I'M THE GIRL WHO THINKS WE CAN USE DR. LIZARD'S NOTES TO RETURN ALL HIS EXPERIMENTS TO NORMAL.
AND I'M ALSO THE GIRL WHO KNOWS YOU'RE PETER PARKER AND MILES MORALES, SO LESS STARING AND MORE SCIENCING.
WHAT? NO WAY! OF COURSE I'M NOT--I MEAN--
YEAH, WE'RE... UTTERLY DIFFERENT PEOPLE THAN... THAN... WHAT YOU SAID. WE'RE, *UH*...
--I'VE NEVER HEARD OF... THOSE GUYS.
COME ON. REALLY? I KNOW YOU GUYS HAVE TRUST ISSUES AND ARE ALWAYS TRYING TO LEAVE ME OUT OF YOUR PLANS, BUT...
WAIT... ARE YOU...
...*GWEN STACY?*

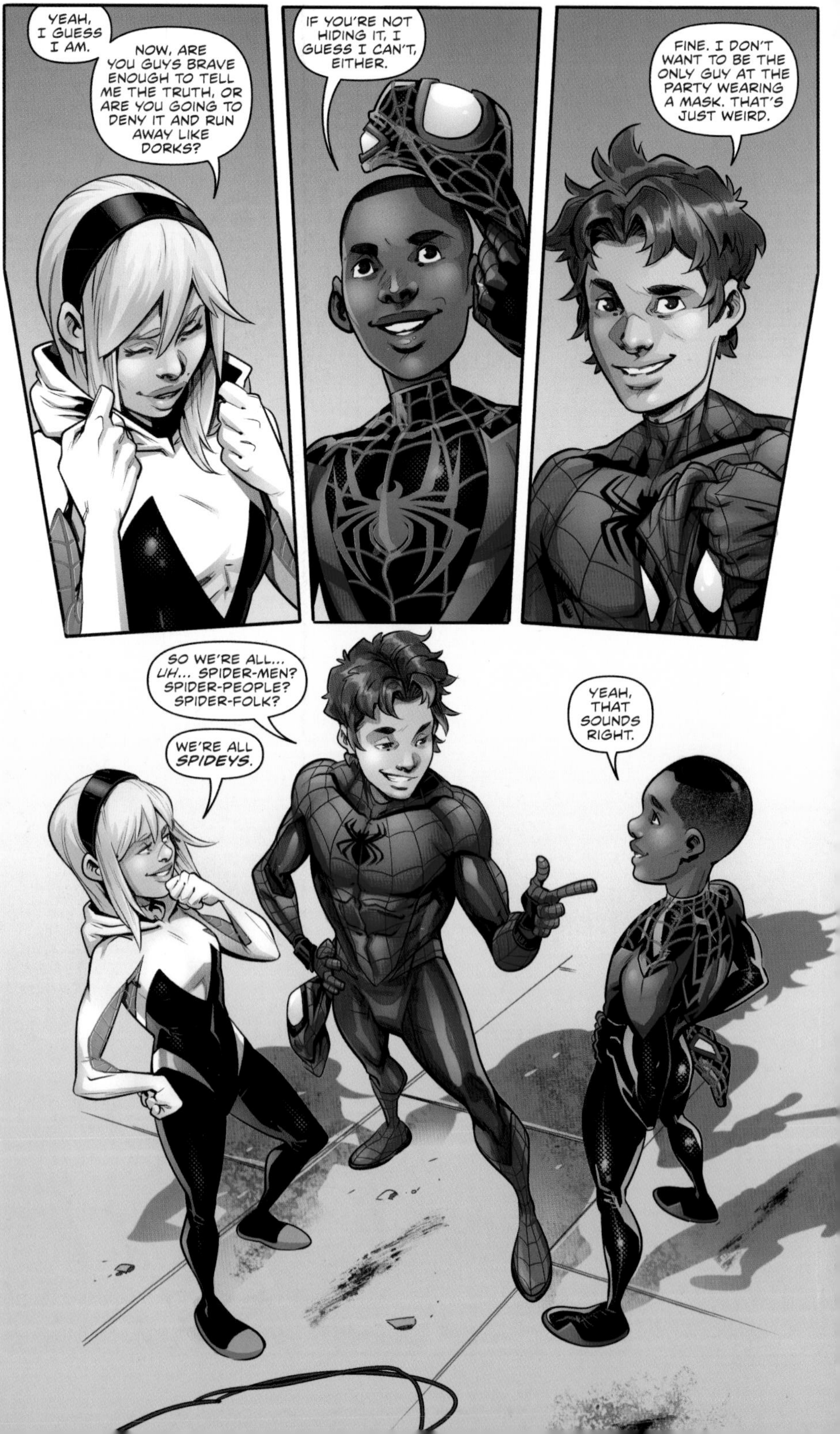
YEAH, I GUESS I AM.
NOW, ARE YOU GUYS BRAVE ENOUGH TO TELL ME THE TRUTH, OR ARE YOU GOING TO DENY IT AND RUN AWAY LIKE DORKS?
IF YOU'RE NOT HIDING IT, I GUESS I CAN'T, EITHER.
FINE. I DON'T WANT TO BE THE ONLY GUY AT THE PARTY WEARING A MASK. THAT'S JUST WEIRD.
SO WE'RE ALL... UH... SPIDER-MEN? SPIDER-PEOPLE? SPIDER-FOLK?
WE'RE ALL SPIDEYS.
YEAH, THAT SOUNDS RIGHT.

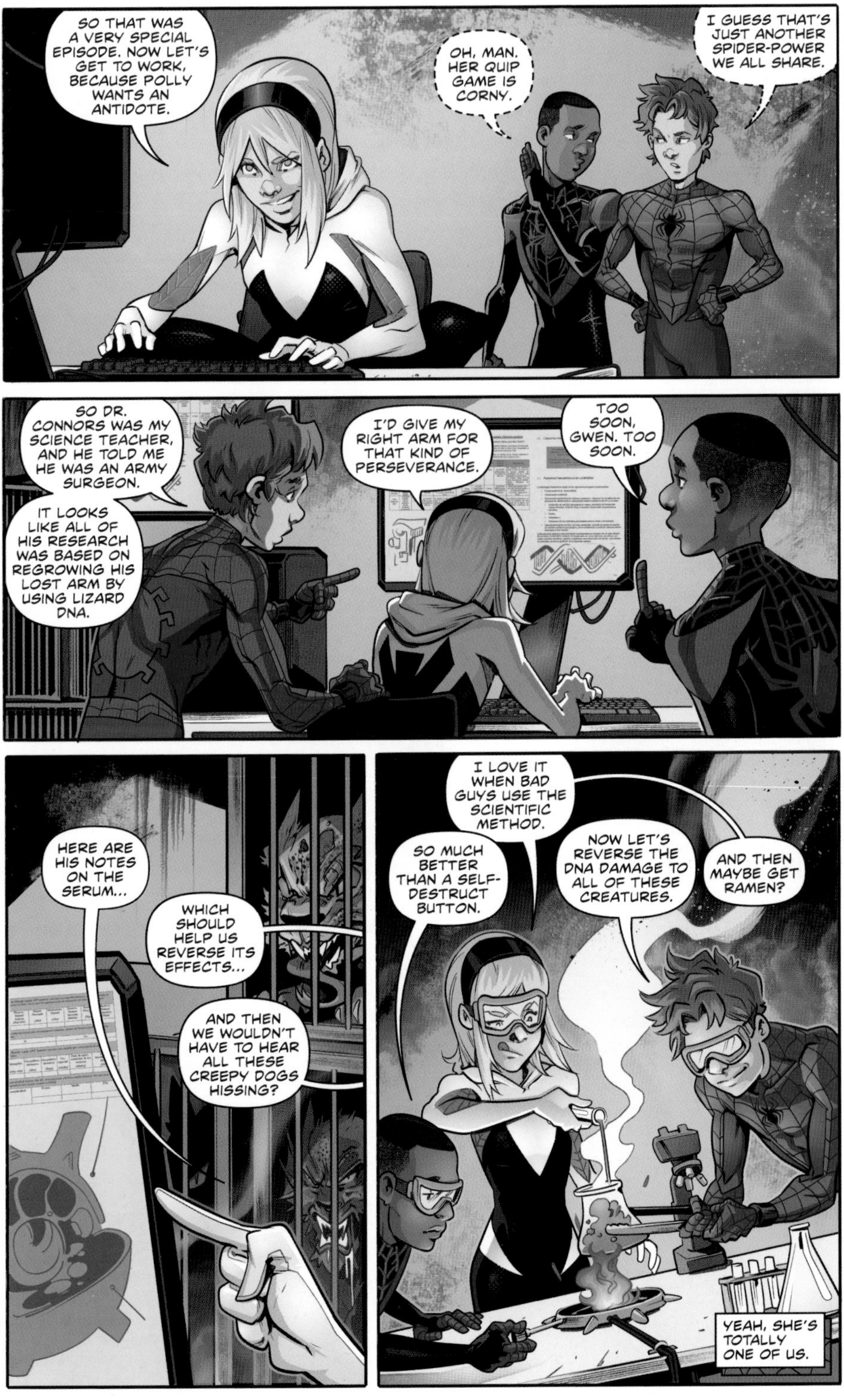
SO THAT WAS A VERY SPECIAL EPISODE. NOW LET'S GET TO WORK, BECAUSE POLLY WANTS AN ANTIDOTE.
OH, MAN. HER QUIP GAME IS CORNY.
I GUESS THAT'S JUST ANOTHER SPIDER-POWER WE ALL SHARE.
SO DR. CONNORS WAS MY SCIENCE TEACHER, AND HE TOLD ME HE WAS AN ARMY SURGEON.
IT LOOKS LIKE ALL OF HIS RESEARCH WAS BASED ON REGROWING HIS LOST ARM BY USING LIZARD DNA.
I'D GIVE MY RIGHT ARM FOR THAT KIND OF PERSEVERANCE.
TOO SOON, GWEN. TOO SOON.
HERE ARE HIS NOTES ON THE SERUM...
WHICH SHOULD HELP US REVERSE ITS EFFECTS...
AND THEN WE WOULDN'T HAVE TO HEAR ALL THESE CREEPY DOGS HISSING?
I LOVE IT WHEN BAD GUYS USE THE SCIENTIFIC METHOD.
SO MUCH BETTER THAN A SELF-DESTRUCT BUTTON.
NOW LET'S REVERSE THE DNA DAMAGE TO ALL OF THESE CREATURES.
AND THEN MAYBE GET RAMEN?
YEAH, SHE'S TOTALLY ONE OF US.

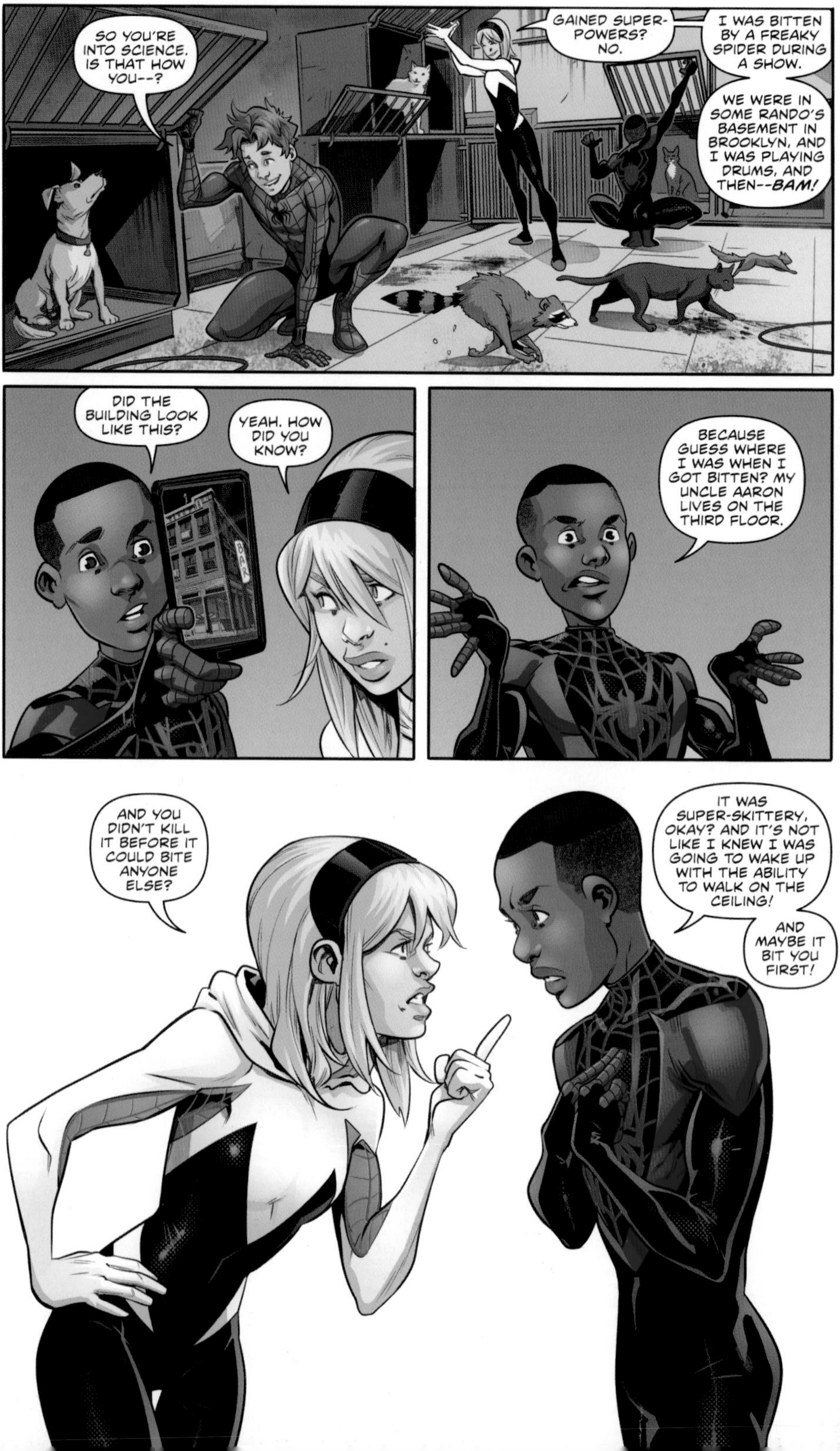

SO YOU'RE INTO SCIENCE. IS THAT HOW YOU--?
GAINED SUPER-POWERS? NO.
I WAS BITTEN BY A FREAKY SPIDER DURING A SHOW.
WE WERE IN SOME RANDO'S BASEMENT IN BROOKLYN, AND I WAS PLAYING DRUMS, AND THEN--BAM!
DID THE BUILDING LOOK LIKE THIS?
BAR
YEAH. HOW DID YOU KNOW?
BECAUSE GUESS WHERE I WAS WHEN I GOT BITTEN? MY UNCLE AARON LIVES ON THE THIRD FLOOR.
AND YOU DIDN'T KILL IT BEFORE IT COULD BITE ANYONE ELSE?
IT WAS SUPER-SKITTERY, OKAY? AND IT'S NOT LIKE I KNEW I WAS GOING TO WAKE UP WITH THE ABILITY TO WALK ON THE CEILING!
AND MAYBE IT BIT YOU FIRST!

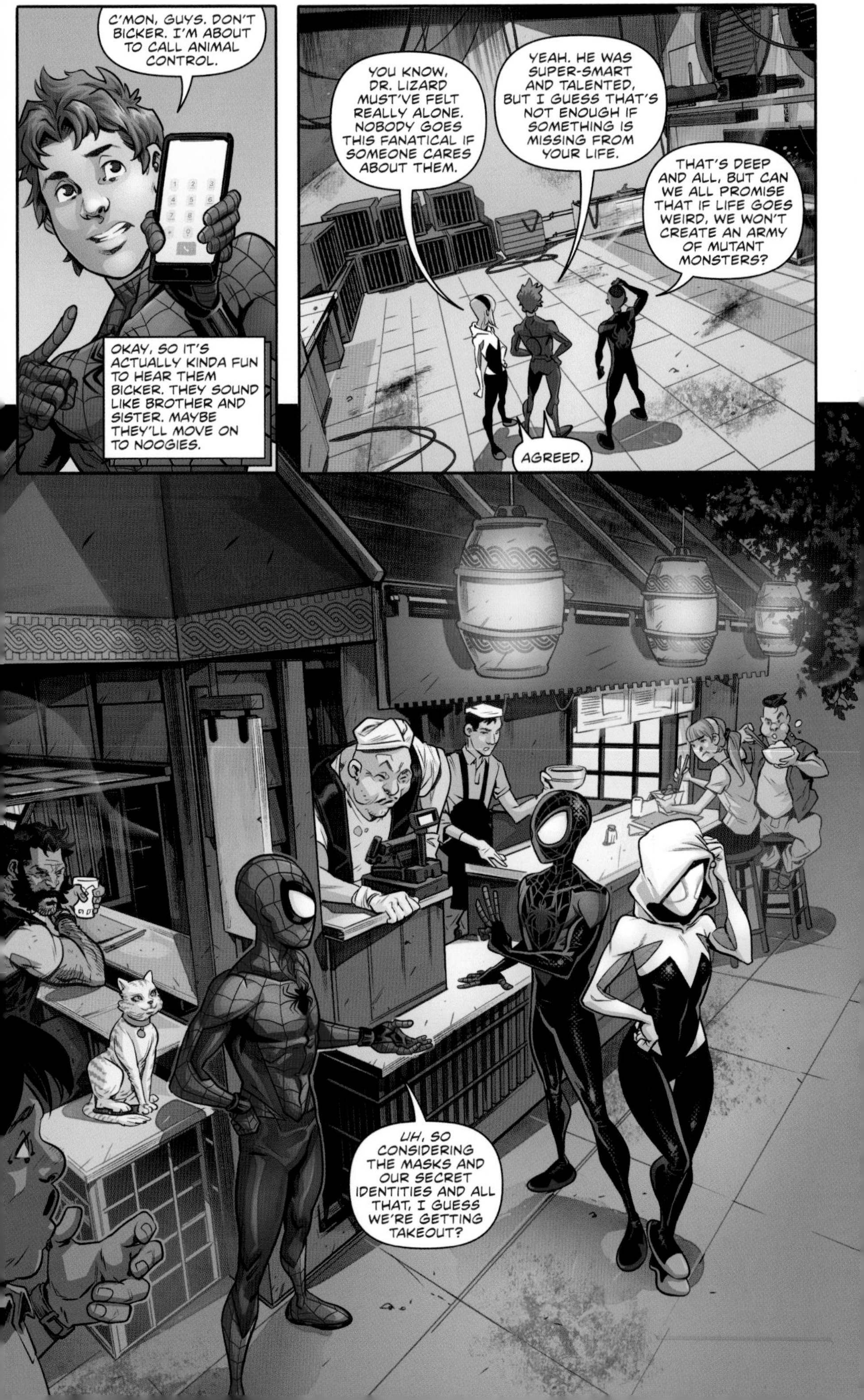

C'MON, GUYS. DON'T BICKER. I'M ABOUT TO CALL ANIMAL CONTROL.
OKAY, SO IT'S ACTUALLY KINDA FUN TO HEAR THEM BICKER. THEY SOUND LIKE BROTHER AND SISTER. MAYBE THEY'LL MOVE ON TO NOOGIES.
YOU KNOW, DR. LIZARD MUST'VE FELT REALLY ALONE. NOBODY GOES THIS FANATICAL IF SOMEONE CARES ABOUT THEM.
YEAH. HE WAS SUPER-SMART AND TALENTED, BUT I GUESS THAT'S NOT ENOUGH IF SOMETHING IS MISSING FROM YOUR LIFE.
THAT'S DEEP AND ALL, BUT CAN WE ALL PROMISE THAT IF LIFE GOES WEIRD, WE WON'T CREATE AN ARMY OF MUTANT MONSTERS?
AGREED.
UH, SO CONSIDERING THE MASKS AND OUR SECRET IDENTITIES AND ALL THAT, I GUESS WE'RE GETTING TAKEOUT?

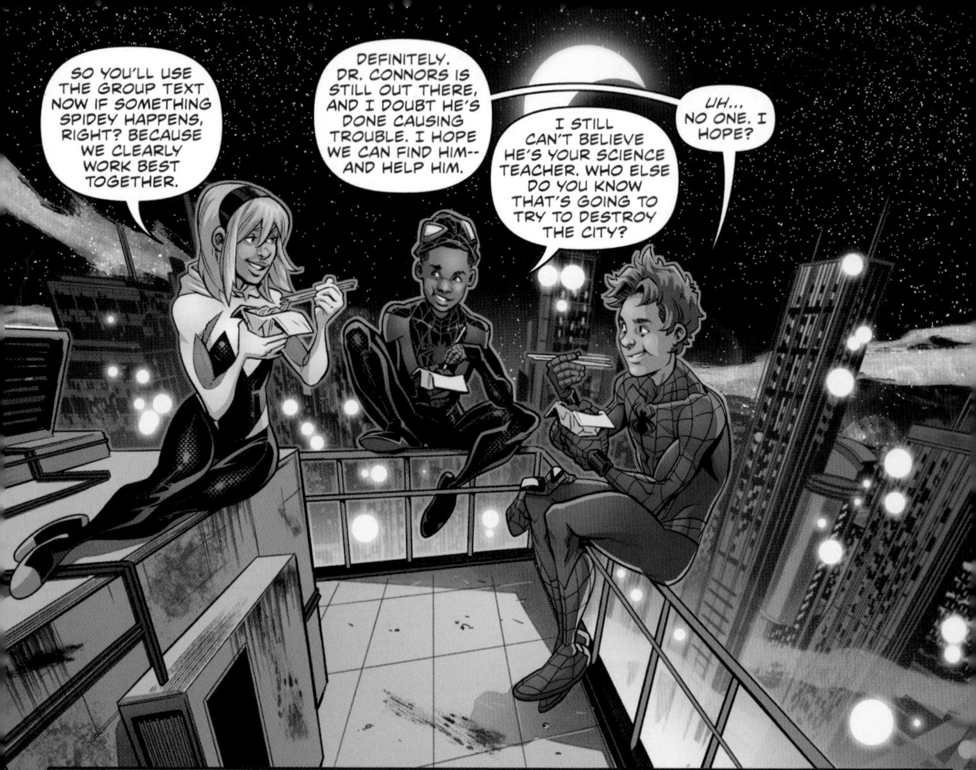
SO YOU'LL USE THE GROUP TEXT NOW IF SOMETHING SPIDEY HAPPENS, RIGHT? BECAUSE WE CLEARLY WORK BEST TOGETHER.
DEFINITELY. DR. CONNORS IS STILL OUT THERE, AND I DOUBT HE'S DONE CAUSING TROUBLE. I HOPE WE CAN FIND HIM-- AND HELP HIM.
I STILL CAN'T BELIEVE HE'S YOUR SCIENCE TEACHER. WHO ELSE DO YOU KNOW THAT'S GOING TO TRY TO DESTROY THE CITY?
UH... NO ONE. I HOPE?

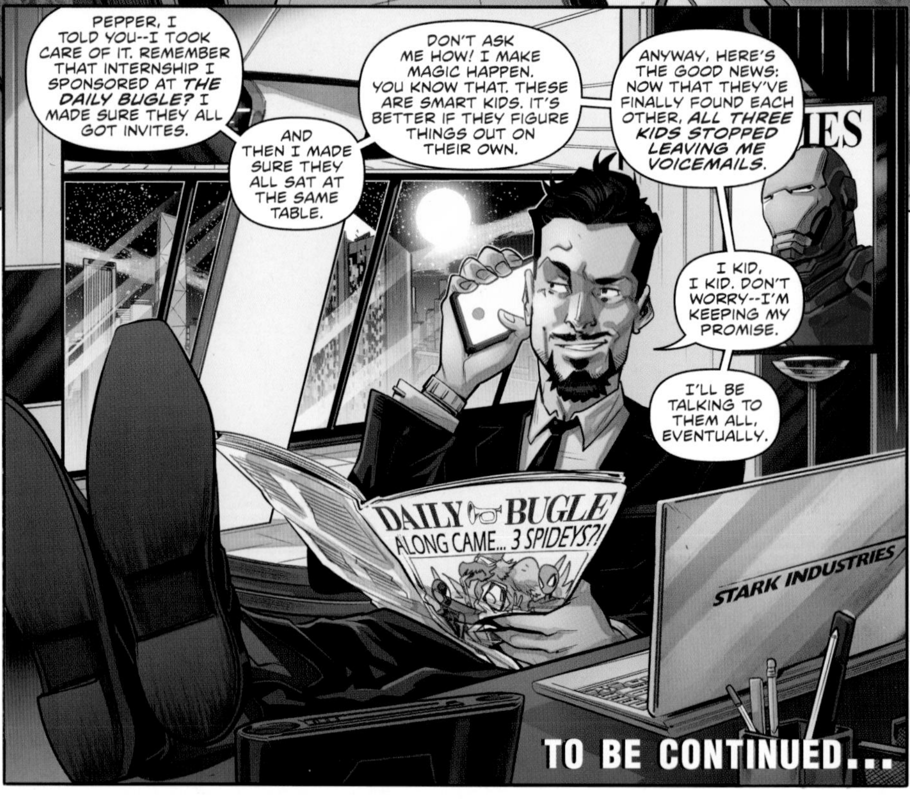
PEPPER, I TOLD YOU--I TOOK CARE OF IT. REMEMBER THAT INTERNSHIP I SPONSORED AT *THE DAILY BUGLE?* I MADE SURE THEY ALL GOT INVITES.
AND THEN I MADE SURE THEY ALL SAT AT THE SAME TABLE.
DON'T ASK ME HOW! I MAKE MAGIC HAPPEN. YOU KNOW THAT. THESE ARE SMART KIDS. IT'S BETTER IF THEY FIGURE THINGS OUT ON THEIR OWN.
ANYWAY, HERE'S THE GOOD NEWS: NOW THAT THEY'VE FINALLY FOUND EACH OTHER, ***ALL THREE KIDS STOPPED LEAVING ME VOICEMAILS.***
I KID, I KID. DON'T WORRY--I'M KEEPING MY PROMISE.
I'LL BE TALKING TO THEM ALL, EVENTUALLY.
DAILY BUGLE
ALONG CAME... 3 SPIDEYS?!
STARK INDUSTRIES
TO BE CONTINUED...

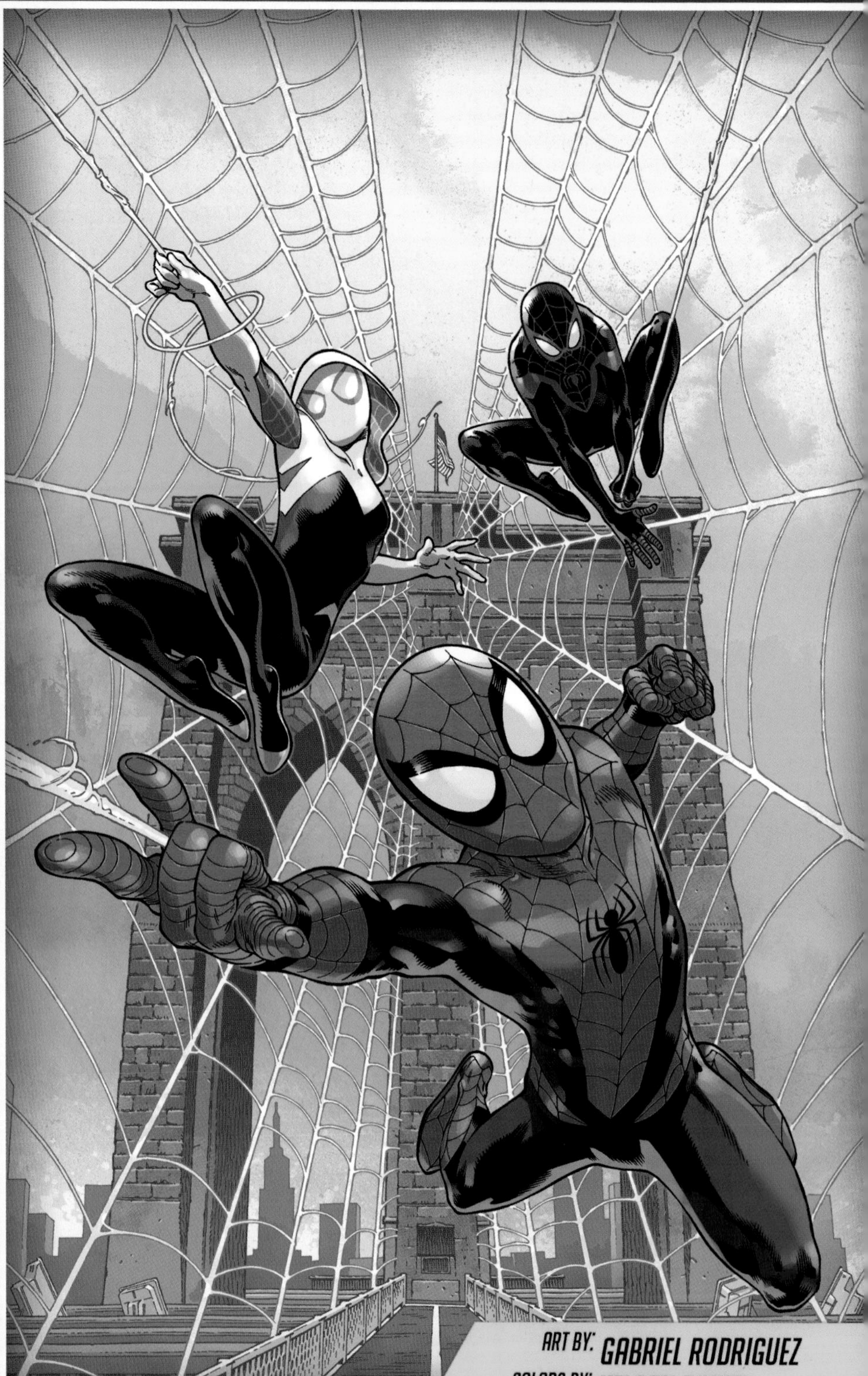
ART BY: GABRIEL RODRIGUEZ
COLORS BY: NELSON DANIEL

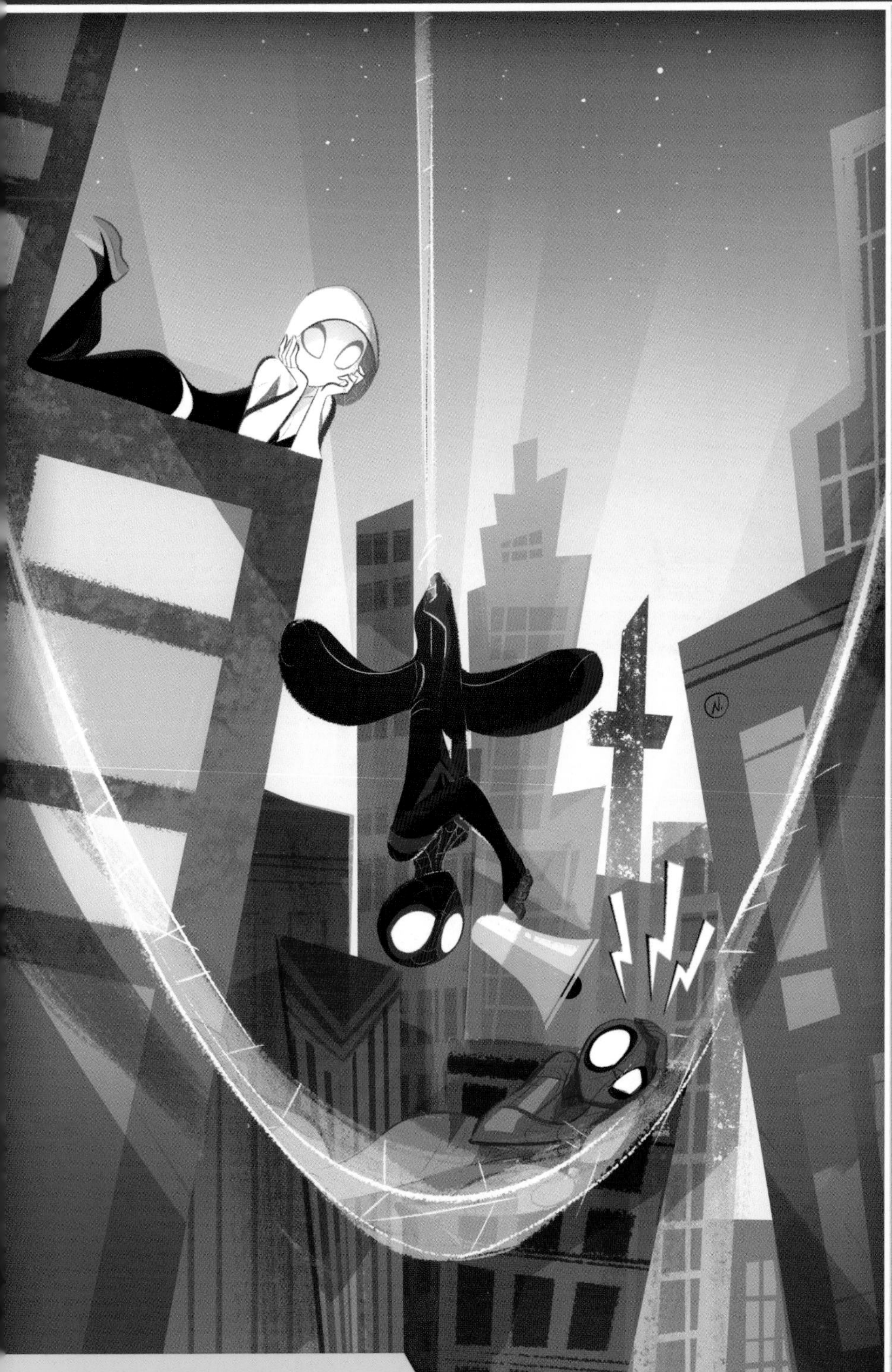

ART BY: NICOLETTA BALDARI

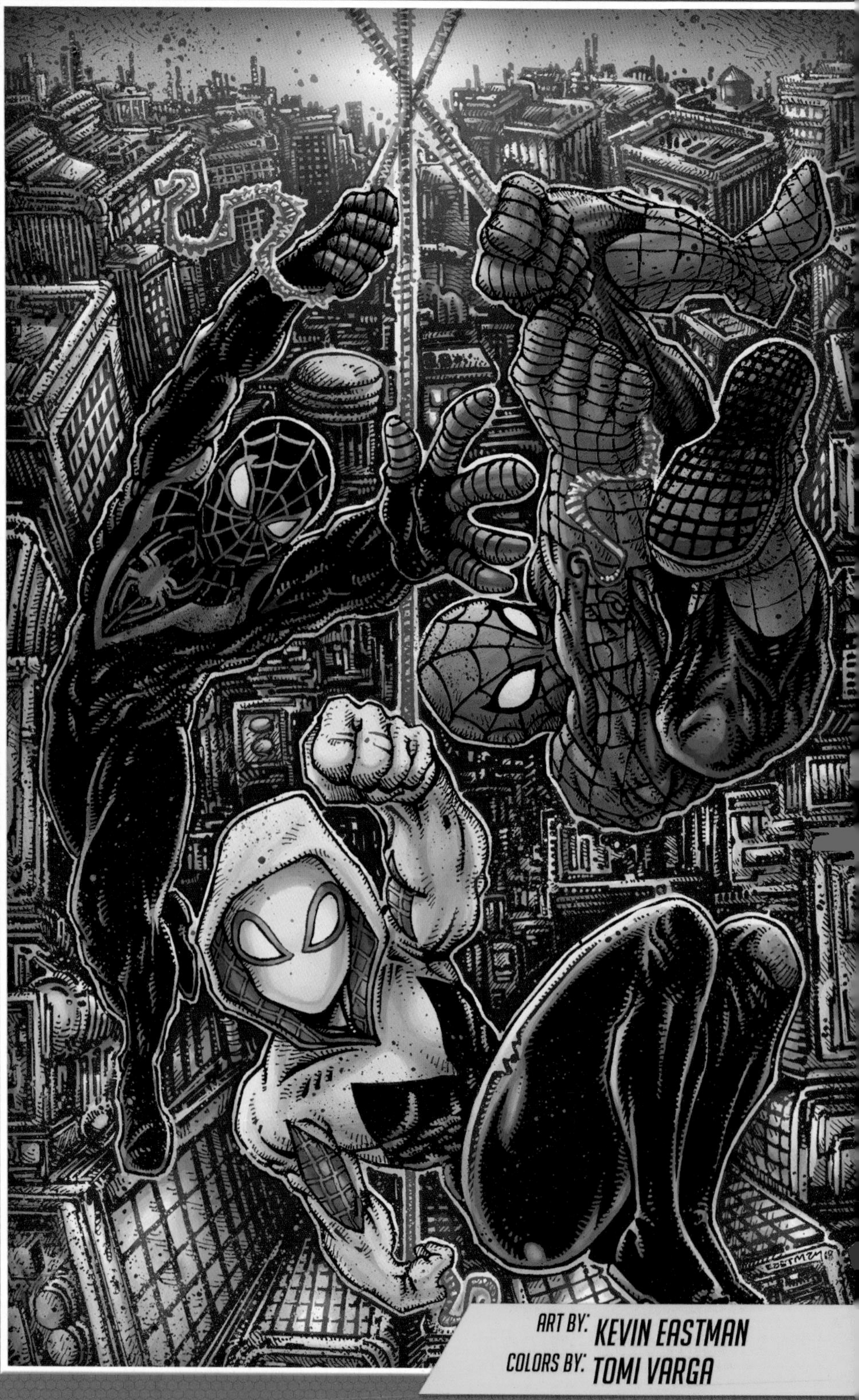

ART BY: KEVIN EASTMAN
COLORS BY: TOMI VARGA

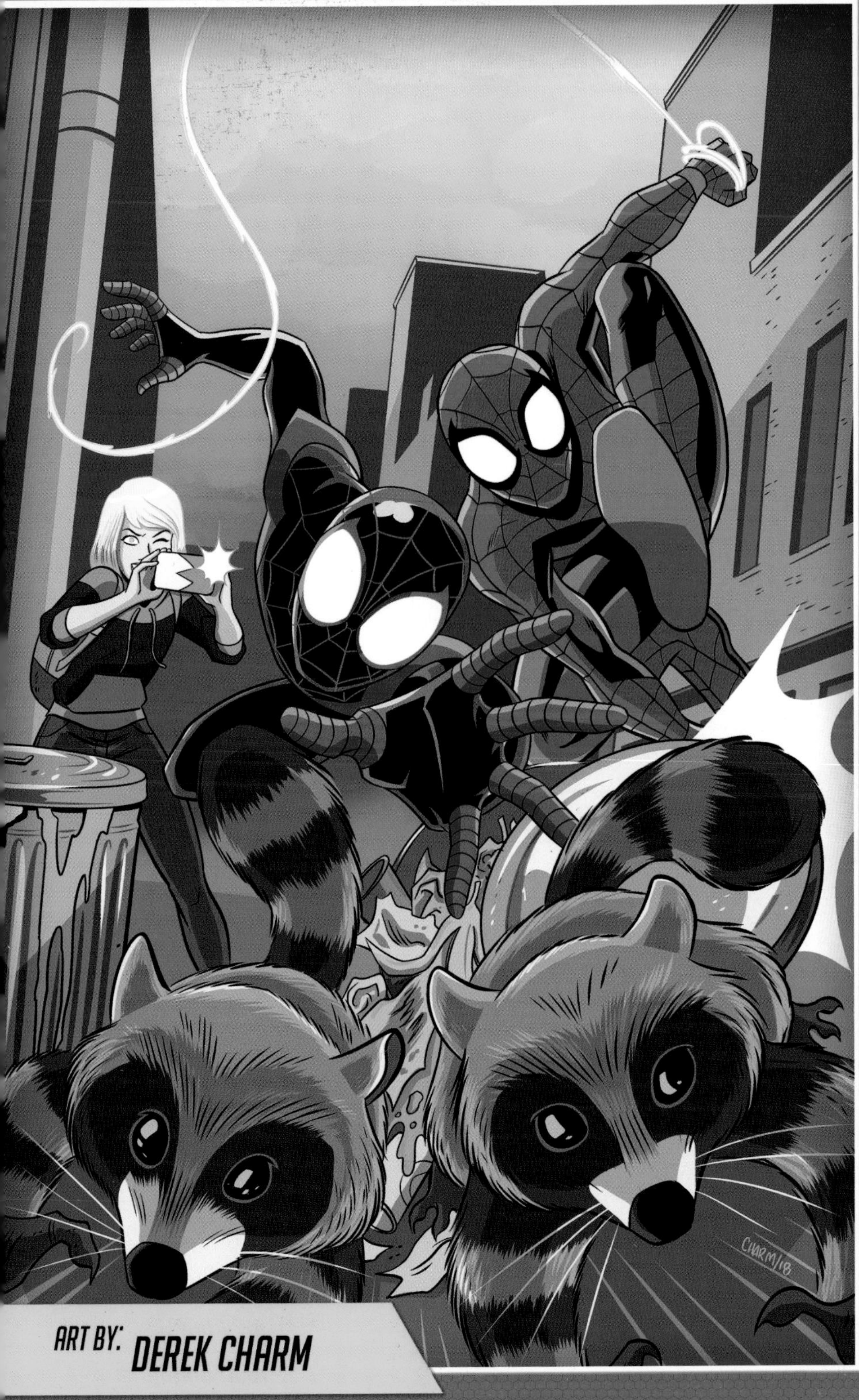
CHARM/18

ART BY: DEREK CHARM

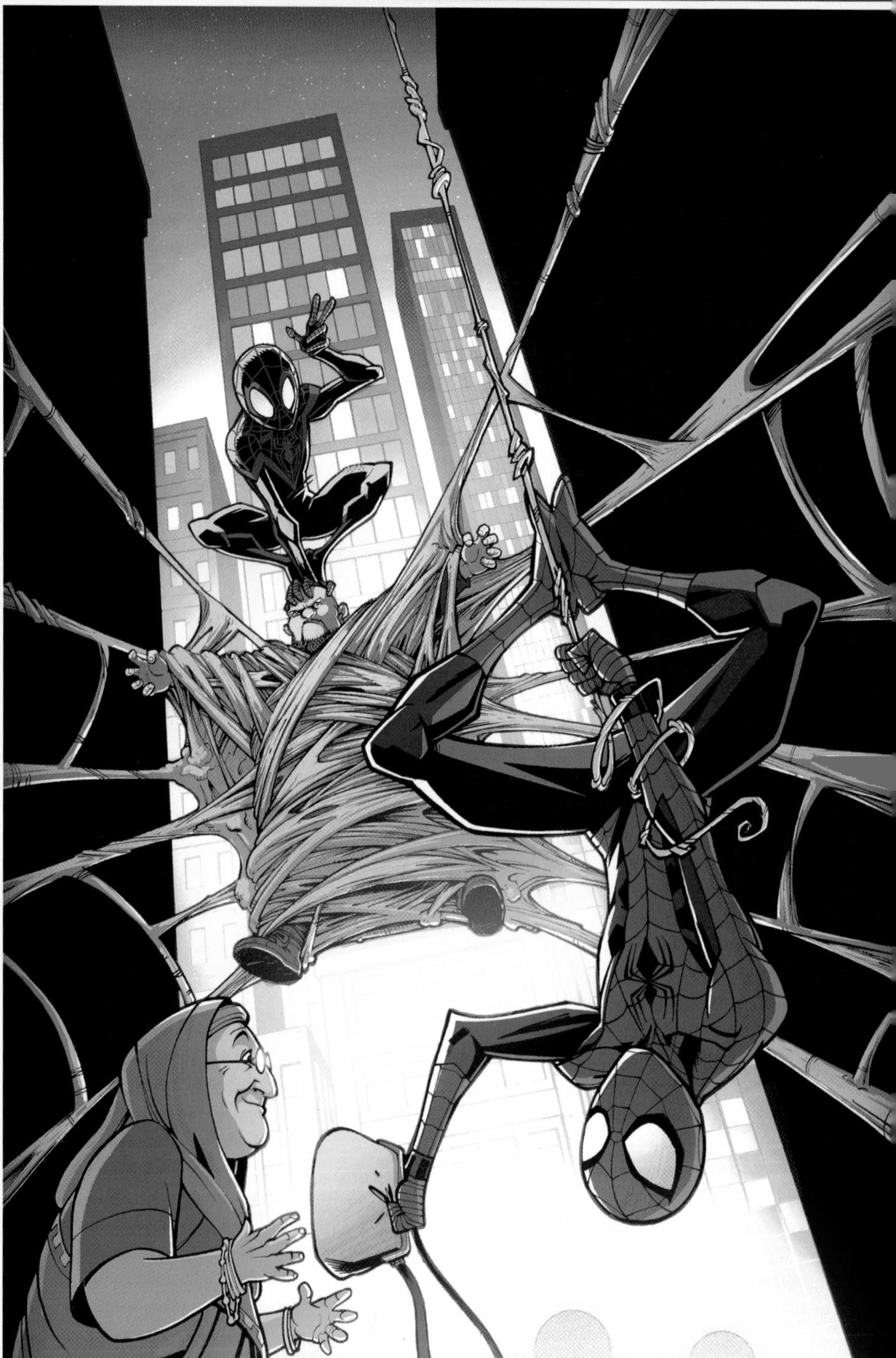

ART BY: NICK ROCHE
COLORS BY: JOSH BURCHAM

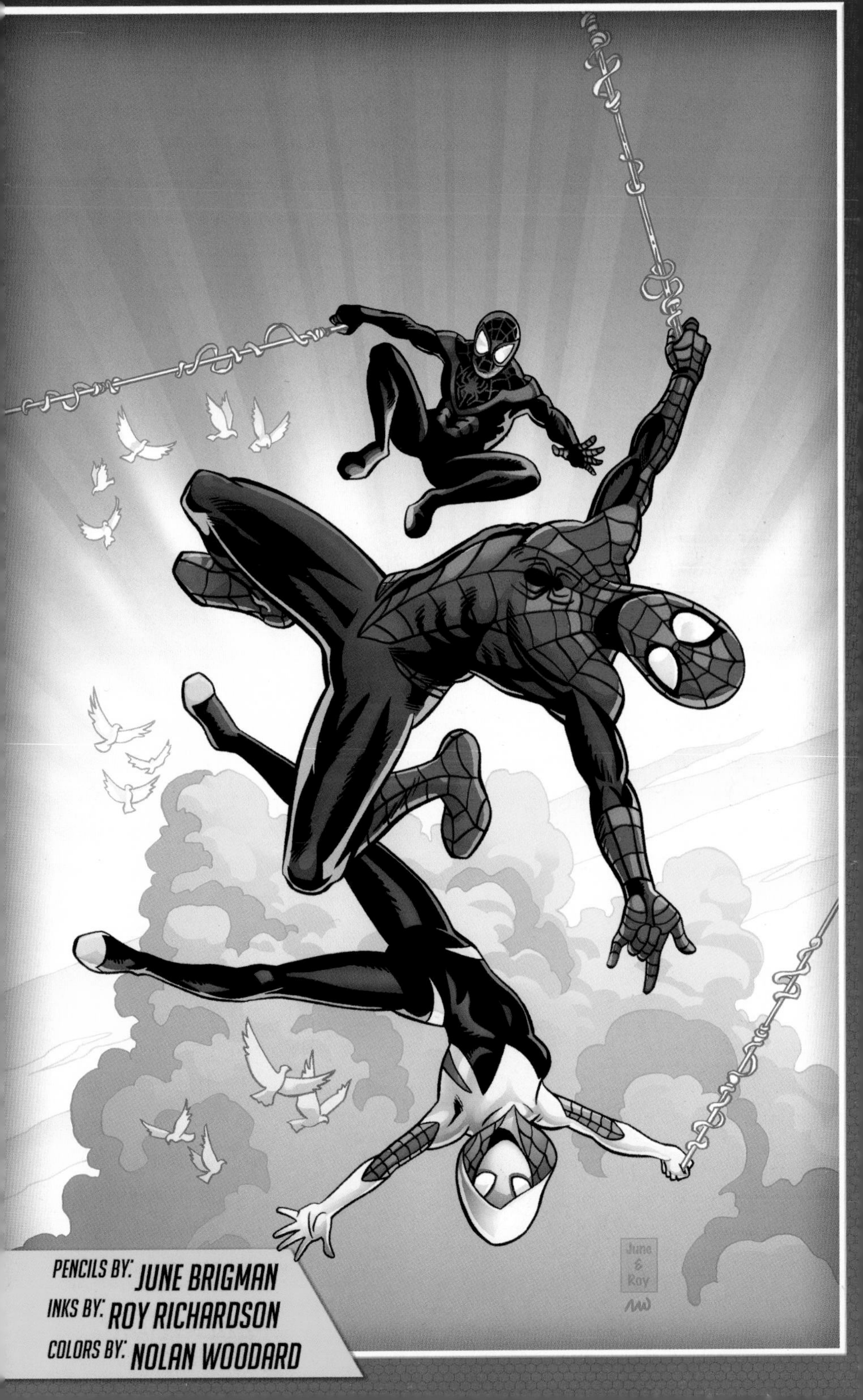
June & Roy

PENCILS BY: JUNE BRIGMAN
INKS BY: ROY RICHARDSON
COLORS BY: NOLAN WOODARD

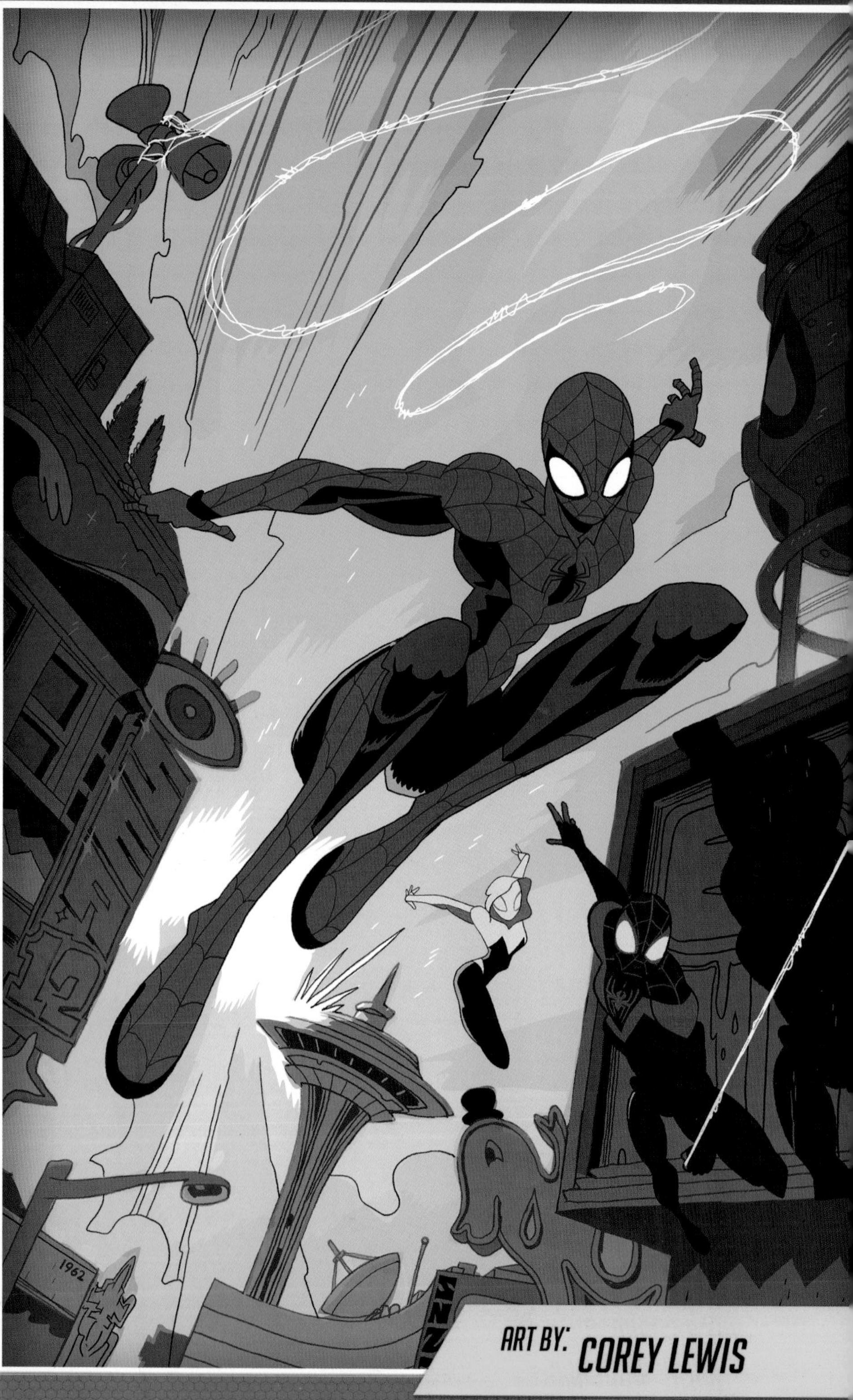
1962

ART BY: COREY LEWIS

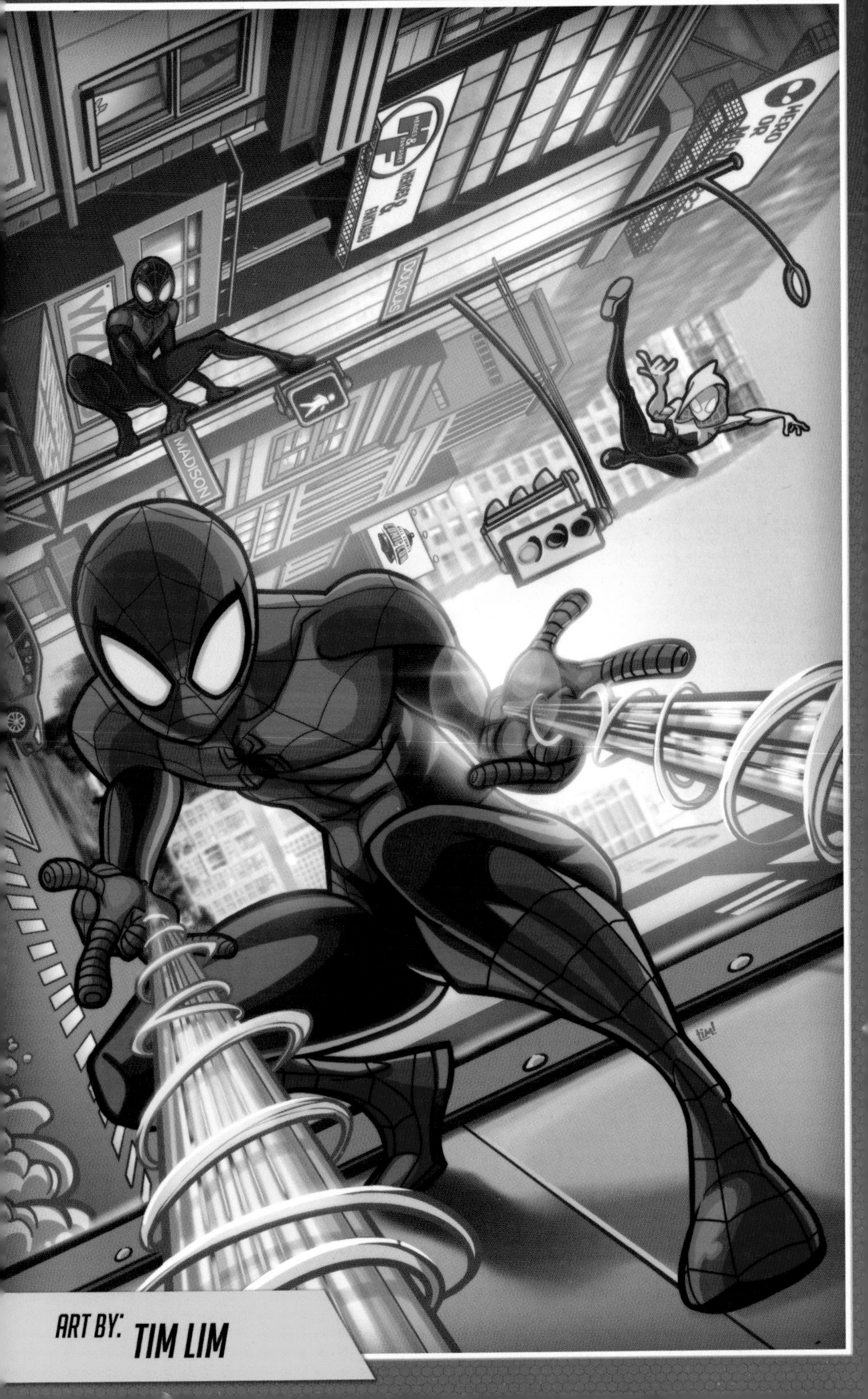
DOUGLAS
MADISON

ART BY: TIM LIM

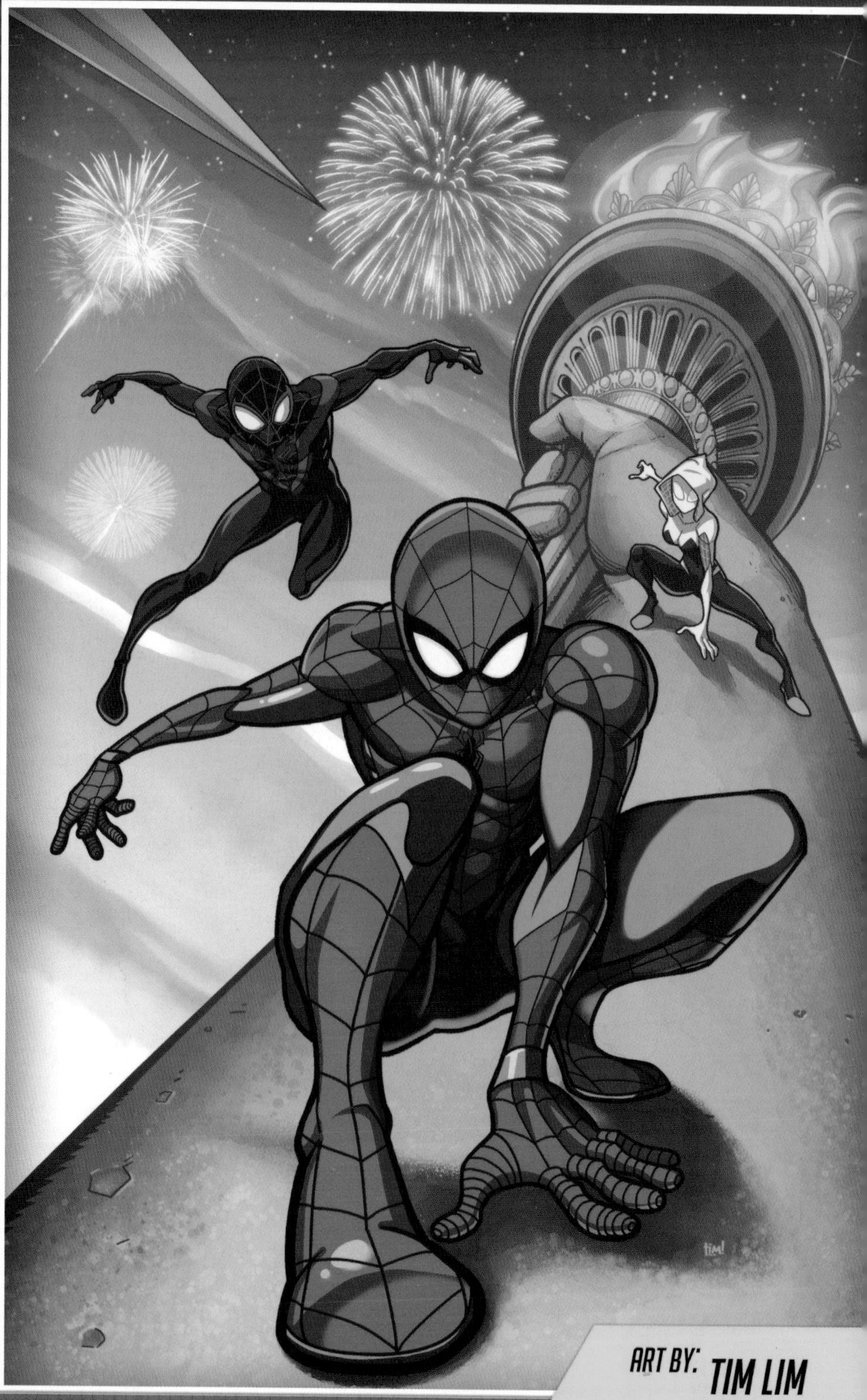
tim!

ART BY: TIM LIM

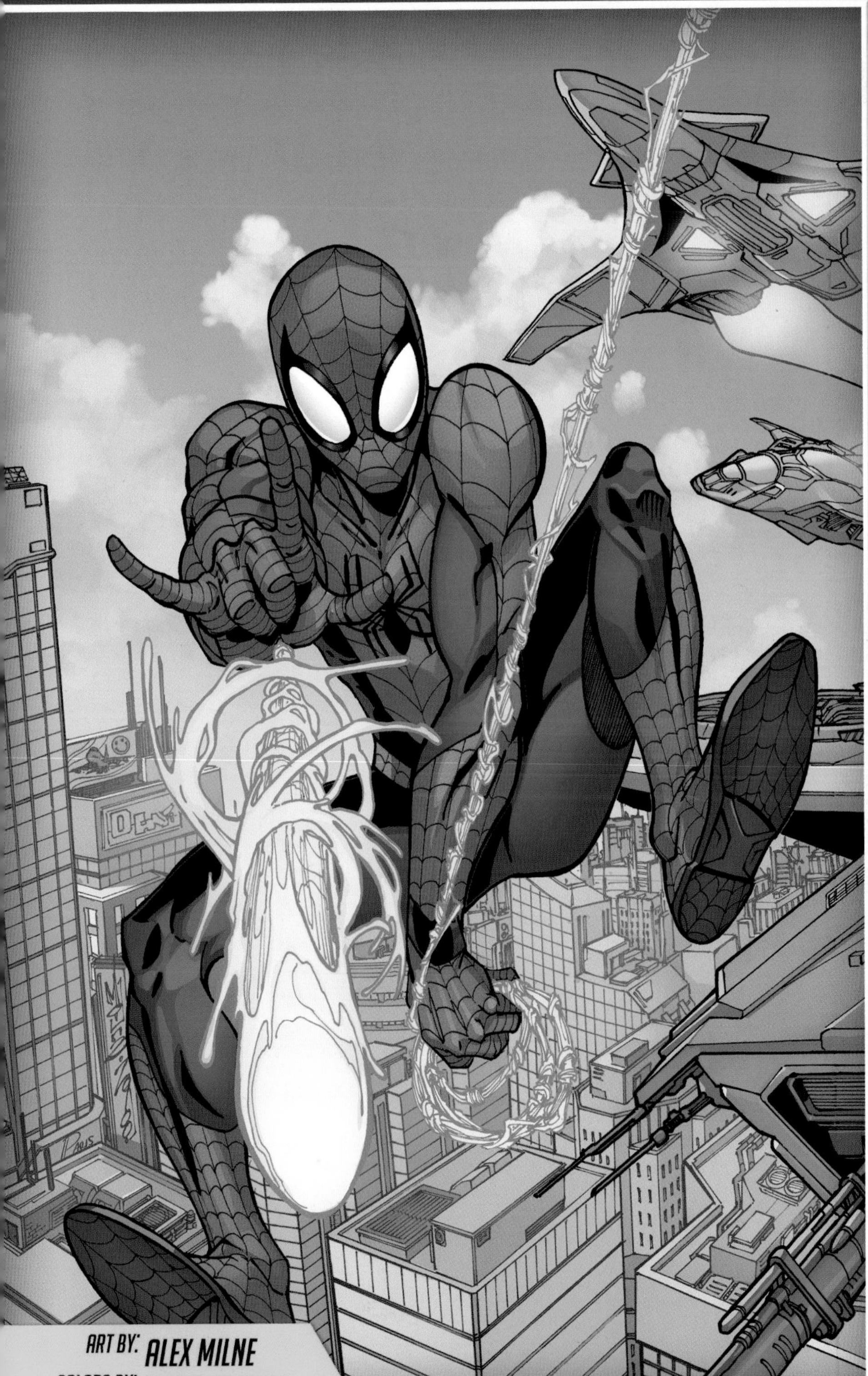

ART BY: ALEX MILNE
COLORS BY: PARIS ALLEYNE

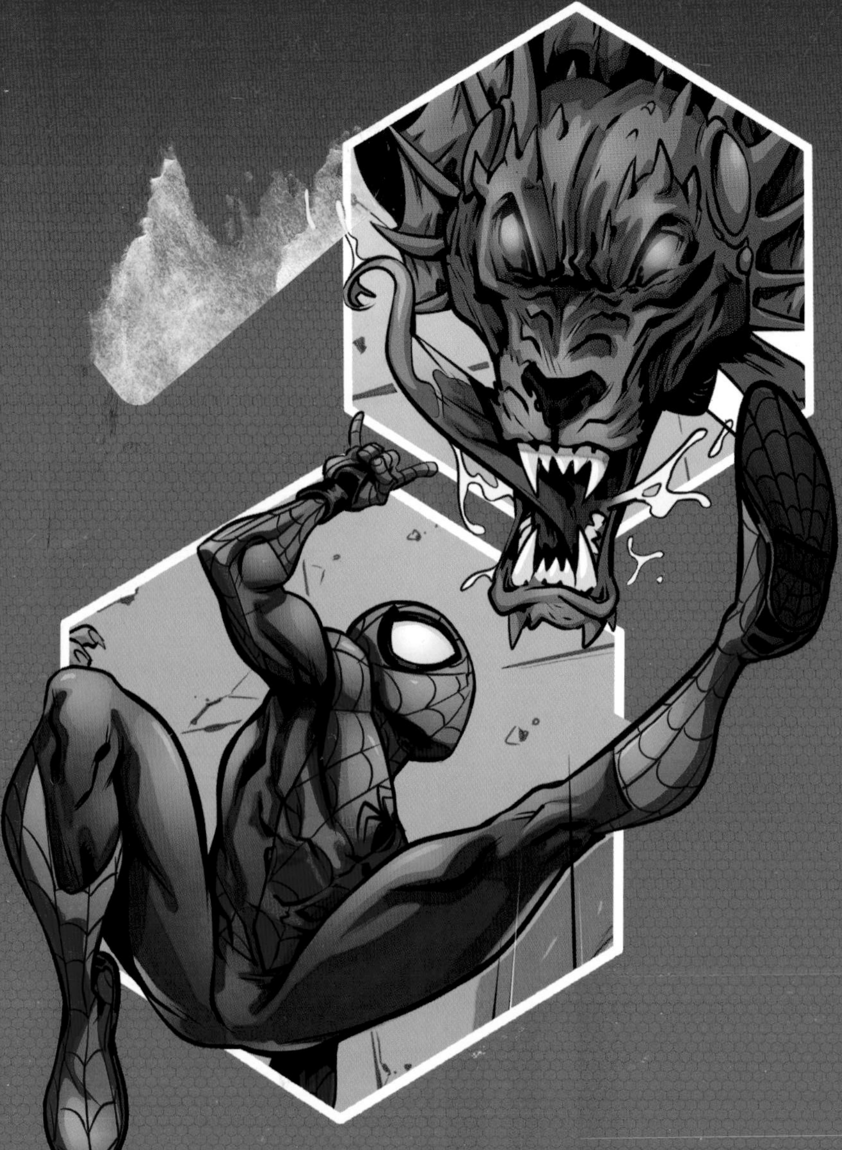